G.I. JOE
ABOVE & BEYOND

Also from Del Rey

G.I. JOE: Rise of Cobra by Max Allan Collins

Max Allan Collins

BALLANTINE BOOKS • NEW YORK

A Del Rey Mass Market Original

Copyright © 2009 by Hasbro Inc. & ® or ™ where indicated.
Copyright © 2009 Paramount Pictures

All Rights Reserved. Used Under Authorization.

Published in the United States by Del Rey, an imprint of The Random House Publishing Group, a division of Random House, Inc., New York.

Del Rey is a registered trademark and the Del Rey colophon is a trademark of Random House, Inc.

G.I. JOE and all related characters are trademarks of Hasbro and are used with permission. © 2009 Hasbro. All rights reserved.

ISBN 978-0-345-51608-4

Printed in the United States of America

www.hasbro.com
www.delreybooks.com

OPM   9 8 7 6 5 4 3 2 1

For those who serve

A TIP OF THE HELMET

I would like to thank Michael Kelly of Hasbro, Inc., for his stellar support, which truly went above and beyond.

Also, thank you to Del Rey editors Tricia Narwani, Susan Moe, and Betsy Mitchell, and to Scott Shannon and Keith Clayton, who first mentioned this project to me at San Diego Comic-Con in 2008—gentlemen, you came through as promised.

Obviously, a big thank-you goes to screenwriters Stuart Beattie and Skip Woods for their fun, action-packed screenplay, *G.I. JOE: The Rise of Cobra,* out of which this prequel was developed.

Finally, a special thanks must go to my frequent collaborator, Matthew Clemens, who helped plot and research this novel. Matt wishes to thank Dave Saleebey, for Washington, D.C., background information.

Readers who enjoy this book are encouraged to seek out *G.I. JOE: The Rise of Cobra*—both the film and the novel.

"Fight till the last gasp."
—WILLIAM SHAKESPEARE

"Courage is resistance to fear,
mastering of fear,
not absence of fear."
—MARK TWAIN

CHAPTER ONE

What Heroes Do

Uzekurkistan

In his white combat suit, Lieutenant Conrad Hauser—Duke to the other nine members of his elite U.S. military covert insertion team—felt like the Michelin tire man. Slogging uphill through nearly knee-deep snow, he was spotlighted by a full moon that shone like a mighty alabaster beacon, illuminating the white-blanketed forest and—most of all, worst of all—the team he led.

Slowly, Duke scanned the tree-covered hilltop, searching for any sign of the Uzekurki troops that he knew would be patrolling this sector.

Nothing.

He lowered his night-vision goggles from his forehead and checked the hill again—still nothing. Nonetheless, in his gut, he felt a twinge of suspicion. He didn't know what caused it, but he had the feeling that danger was imminent, and nearby.

Broad-shouldered yet tall and lean, a white stocking cap covering his close-cropped dark hair, Duke carried his M16 A3 loosely in both hands, safety off, gloved finger on the trigger. Behind him, "Ripcord" Weems—his best friend and second in command—was complaining to the team's medic, David Westen.

Good-natured griping was a specialty of Rip's.

"Why is *he* always out front?" Ripcord asked, loud enough for Duke to hear.

Next to the lanky African American, the slightly built Westen remained stoically quiet. The redhead from Monroe, Louisiana, appeared too frail to keep up with the rest of the team; but the skinny medic had an iron will, and his way of having fun was running twenty miles daily.

Doc was also the only member of the team who spoke even passable Uzekurki.

"We're supposed to be deadly, invisible, and soundless," Duke said, sotto voce. "Emphasis on the *soundless.*"

Undeterred, his voice rising above a strained whisper, Rip asked, "What, you think a brother can't walk point?"

Sliding his night-vision goggles up to his forehead, Duke turned to tell Ripcord to keep it down. Though Rip's kidding riffs could bring a welcome tension break, now was not the time. Exhaling as he turned, watching his breath trail into the frigid night air like wispy smoke, Duke said, "Give it a rest, Rip . . ."

The first bullet whistled past Duke's ear, and he shouted, *"Down,"* even as he dove face-first into the snow. Half a second later, Westen and Rip hit the ground on either side of him, as bullets from up the hill raked the woods around them.

Snow covered Duke's face and the cold stung his

cheeks. He looked first to his left to make sure Westen was okay, then glanced right toward Ripcord, who grinned at him.

"What?" Duke asked, as bullets buzzed like angry insects.

With mock innocence, Rip asked, "Don't you think *I* oughta be the dude in white face?"

"Would you mind cutting the damn comedy long enough to return fire? *Please?*"

The whole team opened up at once, shooting uphill toward the muzzle flashes, where what were presumably Uzekurki troops were hidden by the trees, and dressed in camouflage white, not unlike the Americans.

So much for Duke's team being soundless and invisible—if they were going to get out of this scrape, they'd better get damned deadly damned fast.

The drawbacks of the mission were supposedly offset by the advantage of surprise: parachute in, extract a team of six scientists held hostage in a Uzekurki fortress, beat feet to the extraction point, and get home. It had all sounded routine if dangerous during the briefing. Now, with the Uzekurki patrol pinning them down, Duke was rethinking his definition of what constituted a *routine* mission. . . .

Sneaking a glance up the hill, Duke could see a possible way to outflank the Uzekurki patrol—a long gully ran up the side of the hill, perhaps twenty yards left of his team's position. If a couple men could get to the ravine, and shimmy up the hill, they'd be on level ground with the patrol . . . and that might change the odds.

Duke was hoping the Uzekurkis hadn't made a radio call, either for reinforcements or to alert HQ to the presence of the insertion team. But he knew that was a prayer that would likely go unanswered. . . .

"Rip," Duke shouted over the gunfire, "with me!"

Not waiting for an answer, Duke crawled to his left, the enemy gunfire following him almost as closely as Rip, bullets hissing through snow, splintering trees.

Rip asked, "What the hell are you *doin'*, bro?"

"I thought you said you liked it hot," Duke said.

"*Bikini* women hot," Rip said, "umbrella drinks on the *beach* hot—not up to my butt in snow, bullets flyin' around my *head* hot."

"I take you on a snowy retreat, and all you can do is bitch, bitch, bitch."

"Come on, Duke—you know we don't *never* retreat. . . ."

Duke stopped, Ripcord right behind him, the two as flat as possible in the snow, the Uzekurki patrol still peppering the world around them with gunfire, although the return fire from Duke's team had the Uzekurkis keeping their heads down some now themselves.

Using his com-link system to the team, Duke said, "All right, guys, cover fire while Rip and I hotfoot it up the hill."

A torrent of "Yes, sirs," and "Got its" followed as the whole team seemed to answer at once.

"You ready?" Duke asked.

"Ready for what exactly?" Rip asked, but it was too late for details.

In one motion, Duke rose and sprinted toward the gully. Into his com link, he shouted, *"Now!"*

Instantly, the team's rate of fire up the hill increased, although the Uzekurkis continued to blast downhill, as well. Even over the clatter of gunfire, Duke could hear Rip's footsteps crunching in the snow behind him. Bullets continued to fly all around, and Duke had the fleeting thought that the Uzekurki army must be the worst shots on the planet, which was fine with him. Hundreds of Uzekurki rounds sent their way, and neither he nor Rip had so much as a scratch. Some freaking marksmen.

Diving into the gully, Rip sliding on his six, Duke rolled into the trunk of a tree, the impact knocking the air from him just as Rip crashed into him from the other side.

As he came up, ready to fire, Duke said, "I don't need to worry about the Uzekurkis—*you're* going to kill me first."

With a little grin, Rip said, "Thanks for breaking my fall, buddy."

Both men now had their weapons trained uphill as they crept through the underbrush of the ravine. No trail here, and each step had to be taken carefully to avoid sinking into the snow. Between the gun smoke and the misty breath of the combatants, a fog enveloped the hillside, making it difficult to see, even in the gully where Duke and Rip hunkered.

Duke whispered as loudly as he dared: "Let's get up that damn hill."

"Right behind you, bro," Rip said as they edged up the gully, weaving between trees.

They had moved less than a hundred yards up the ravine when a Uzekurki soldier popped up, not even fifty yards away. Duke brought up his weapon and fired once, the bullet striking the Uzekurki in the forehead and dropping him in the snow.

As they watched the soldier's last breath evaporate over his corpse, two of his comrades materialized behind him and leveled their weapons at Duke and Rip. The one on the right got off a round, the bullet striking Duke in the chest, knocking him back. As he fell, he saw Ripcord drop both Uzekurkis—one shot each to the forehead.

Duke felt like a truck had hit him as he lay in the snow, the night sky above him, the stars twinkling their gentle laughter as he tried to draw a breath.

Another thing to reassess now: Uzekurki marksmanship.

"You okay?" Rip asked, kneeling over him.

Looking up at his friend, his vision slightly blurring from the painful jolt the bullet delivered smashing into his body armor, Duke said, "No thanks to you."

"Hey," Rip whined. "I dropped *both* them suckers."

"Not until after one shot me."

"Yeah, but he shot you in your armor."

Duke stared up at Rip. "*That's* your excuse? That the idiot didn't try for a head shot?"

"With your head, it'd take armor-piercing."

"Help me up before any more of 'em show. Getting shot once per mission is once more than acceptable."

Helping Duke to his feet, Rip said, "Nobody likes a complainer, bro."

Duke was about to respond to this outrageous assertion when three more members of the Uzekurki patrol rose, seemingly from nowhere, and leveled their weapons at the American pair. Duke and Rip faced each other, Duke's weapon pointed downhill, Rip's at the Uzekurkis, but barrel down.

"Damn," the two men said.

One of the Uzekurki soldiers said something unintelligible, which Duke translated roughly as, "Drop your guns and put your hands up."

"Now look what you did," Rip said.

Duke frowned. "What *I* did?"

The Uzekurki soldier repeated his order louder and angrier.

The last syllable still hung in the air as Rip's M16 came up and he sprayed the trio of Uzekurkis, Duke rolling to his left and coming up firing. One Uzekurki managed to fire a round impotently skyward before he fell next to his equally dead compatriots.

Without further banter, Duke and Rip hustled up the hill to find themselves on the right flank of the enemy position, maybe thirty yards away, only a half-dozen members of the patrol remaining.

With a quick mutual nod, they opened fire and, in seconds, it was over.

After a hasty preliminary search of the bodies, Duke determined which was the radioman, his equipment shot to hell. The question now was whether or not the radioman had made a call . . . and, if so, what he had reported. . . .

Duke had no desire to wait around to see who showed up to check on the patrol. This little gunfight would force them to alter their route to the fortress now, too.

The original plan had been to come at the objective from the east, using a series of abandoned tunnels, from some long-forgotten conflict, to gain entry from beneath. That plan was probably as dead as the Uzekurki patrol. They had a backup plan, of course.

Unlike the villains' lairs in the war movies and spy flicks Duke had grown up on, this one was not carved into a mountainside—and instead of an ancient castle, the facility was completely modern, occupying the center of a large plain on the other side of the woods.

What awaited them now was lots of open ground to cross, motion detectors, barbed wire, machine guns, and a hundred Uzekurki soldiers.

Westen gave the insertion team a quick once-over, especially Duke, but everyone had come through the firefight unscathed. They took five minutes to check the bodies of the Uzekurki patrol, and get their adrenaline under control again.

"Let's move," Duke said, and the team immediately fell in behind him.

As they swept farther north through the woods, Rip gave their target a yet-wider berth, doing even more to avoid Uzekurki patrols.

Rather than approach the complex from the east,

Duke led the team through the forest, halting at the edge of the woods, north of the facility, a silver-dollar–shaped steel-walled fortress rising from the snow, spread out before them in the middle of the wide-open plain. The first gray hint of dawn appeared, though it'd be awhile before they had sunlight to worry about.

The fortress might be vulnerable to an aerial assault, but anything from the ground they would see coming from hundreds of yards. The forest had been cleared for half a mile all around the complex. Two-lane highways ran from the facility in the four compass directions, interrupting the surrounding blanket of white.

Through the trees that protected them now, across the plain, beyond the complex, Duke could see the floodlights of helicopters sweeping the opposite tree line, vainly searching. More helicopters buzzed around on the east and west, their lights flitting through the trees, the rotors chopping the air, the sound rolling over the plain like threatening thunder.

Above the team, two helicopters droned back and forth, their floodlights arcing through the treetops but never catching the team, the choppers' downdrafts kicking up snow in the faces of Duke and his men when they wandered too close.

"You want us to take them out?" Rip asked over the noise, as a helicopter headed away from them to the west.

Duke shook his head and pointed. "Why not just go out there and wave a flag?"

Rip started patting the pockets of his white uniform. "I might even have one in here somewhere."

Before Duke could top Rip's quip, a gate opened in the complex, and a line of four semi-trailers pulled out and headed west, toward the forest.

"What the hell's that?" Rip asked.

Duke checked for the positions of the helicopters, then trained his binoculars on the convoy of trucks that rolled slowly along, exhaust making white clouds.

Rip frowned. "Are they sending more troops after us?"

"No—those are cargo haulers. Either they're empty because they just brought supplies, or they're full because the complex is shipping something out."

"What would they be shipping out of a fortress?"

Duke gave up a mildly disgusted smirk. "Were you even *at* the briefing?"

Rip looked at him blankly.

"The Uzekurkis are holding a group of scientists whose specialties all relate to weapons development. What do you *suppose* they're shipping out?"

"Weapons maybe?"

Duke touched a gloved fingertip to his nose.

"Hell, then," Rip said, "we should stop 'em."

As the trucks disappeared into the woods, Duke said, "Two problems with that. First, our mission is the *scientists*, not the weapons. Second, they're a mile or more away . . . and we're on foot."

Rip was still formulating a reply when another gate opened at the complex, and a smaller, straight-bed truck rolled out, canvas covering the cargo area, this time to the north and heading their way.

"More troops?" asked Pete Bergman, a tall, muscular soldier from DeKalb, Illinois. A crack rifleman and radioman, Bergman—his brown hair barely past the stubble stage and his eyes an unusually pale blue—could also drive or start anything with a motor, whether he had the key or not.

Shrugging, Duke said, "Maybe, maybe not. Let's saddle up, just in case."

Still mindful of the choppers circling, the team gathered its equipment and prepared to move out.

"What could it be," Rip asked, "besides more troops lookin' for us?"

"That," Duke said, "is what we're going to find out."

"We?" Rip asked.

"You, me, Bergman, and two more," Duke said. "Phelps and Stearns, you guys with us. Westen, you and the rest stay here."

"Roger that," Westen said.

"You always wanna be on point, Rip," Duke said. "Well, it's all yours."

"Oh, *now* you wanna put the brother out front?"

"You're the 'man,' right? Isn't that what you always say? Who better on point?"

Rip's smile was as cool as the weather. "Hate to admit you bein' right about anything, Duke . . . but you're right about this. I'll take point."

Phelps, an African American slightly smaller than a Hummer, fell in behind Ripcord. Next to Phelps, Stearns—a crew-cut former high school

All-American quarterback—carried (in addition to the M16 slung over his shoulder) a handheld rocket launcher. Bergman fell in behind with Duke riding drag.

Snaking through the trees, Rip led them farther west, toward the road, then down a hill where they had a good view.

Once out of sight of the complex, the truck with the canvas-enclosed cargo area pulled off the main road and onto a flattened, snow-covered path. Three Uzekurki soldiers piled out of the cab.

They were not wearing the camouflage white of the patrol the team had met earlier, but rather the green-gray uniforms of the Uzekurki army. A pair went to the rear of the truck and lowered the tailgate.

Three more Uzekurkis climbed down from the truck bed, then turned and waved their guns. Slowly, one at a time, six more people—four men and two women—climbed down. They all wore white lab coats, but Duke doubted the coats were for camouflage. Unless he missed his guess, Duke realized that the scientists were being delivered to them on a silver platter.

The only downside? The six Uzekurki soldiers seemed to be lining the scientists up to shoot them. . . .

Six soldiers and five members of the insertion team, Duke thought.

The odds weren't bad, but Duke didn't want this to turn into a firefight, not with the complex less than a mile away, with God only knew how many Uzekurki soldiers garrisoned there. Well, not only

God knew: so did intel, which had told him more than one hundred.

The scientists were now lined up against some trees, the soldiers in a five-man row about twenty yards away. One soldier stood off to one side, obviously the commander.

Using hand signals, Duke assigned targets to his team. The one nearest the commander, and the commander himself, would be Duke's.

The commander raised an arm and shouted an order that probably translated as "Ready!"

Duke's team steadied its weapons and aimed.

As the commander shouted "Aim!" in Uzekurki, Duke slowly let out a long, slow breath and centered himself.

When the commander opened his mouth to shout, "Fire," Duke shot him through it, blood mist haloing the startled, dying man.

The Uzekurki troops froze, eyes streaking to their commander as his hands went to his throat. Before they could move, all five were shot once in the head, and fell dead in an ungainly sprawl.

Duke was sure the shots were so close together that anyone at the fortress who heard them would simply think the firing squad had carried out its orders.

One scientist screamed; Rip rushed the short distance to the woman and covered her mouth with his hand, firmly but not roughly, whispering something in her ear.

Phelps, Stearns, and Bergman checked the bodies of the firing squad while Duke joined Rip with the hostages.

As Rip removed his hand from the scientist's mouth, Duke looked squarely at the woman. "Are you all right?"

She was a blonde in her midforties, maybe five four, and her eyes were wide with terror, even as Rip's voice soothed her. He backed away slightly.

"Are you all right?" Duke repeated.

The woman nodded without speaking.

"Are you Dr. Elaine Mossman?"

Another nod.

Crisply Duke said, "We're an American military force sent here to get you out. You need to follow my instructions with no discussion, and as quickly as possible."

The scientists had no objection, all overwhelmingly relieved; but they seemed to know that they were far from being out of the woods—both literally and figuratively.

Duke ticked off the names of the other scientists, and each answered in the affirmative, like a student during roll call.

"Easier than we thought," Rip said with a grin.

Duke frowned at him.

Rip lapsed into an injured silence.

But Duke glared at his buddy, who—finally unable to take it—said, "All right, all right," took a few steps to a tree, and knocked on wood, rapping his knuckles on the bark. "How can a grown man be so damn *superstitious*?"

"Not superstitious," Duke said. "Just careful."

Waving the rest of the team over from its position up the hill, Duke was already formulating a plan for their escape to the extraction point.

The original plan had called for blowing up the complex, once the scientists were in their charge. Now that they weren't going into the complex, Duke had to quickly come up with a Plan B.

"What now?" Rip asked.

Duke nodded toward the truck. "Take that sucker, and run like hell."

Westen asked, "Don't you think they'll come after us?"

"Absolutely they'll come after us. In fact, it shouldn't be too long before they start wondering what happened to the firing squad, and send someone out to check. If we're not moving by then, we'll be in very deep, very brown water."

Westen's eyes were tight. "Can we outrun them?"

"Nope," Duke said.

The medic's face screwed up in confusion. "I don't think I understand. . . ."

"You and the team will accompany the scientists in the truck . . . meanwhile, Rip, Stearns, and I will hold off the Uzekurkis."

Ripcord's eyes went wide. " 'Meanwhile'? What's this, a damn comic book?"

"Got a better idea?" Duke asked.

No one spoke up.

Then Westen said to Duke, "I should go with you, Lieutenant."

"Don't be funny."

Westen shook his head. "If anything goes wrong, you're going to need a medic, and there won't be anything funny about it."

Duke sighed, his breath visible; then he nodded. "You make a hell of a point, Doc . . . but which one of these others can speak even one word of Uze-kurki?"

"None of them," Westen admitted.

"Then you go with them." Turning to Stearns and pointing at the rocket launcher, Duke asked, "How many rockets do you have for that thing?"

"Three."

Phelps chimed in, "I've got two more," and he handed them over to Rip.

"Five rockets," Rip bemoaned, "and three M16s . . . perfect for the Fourth of July in Pough-keepsie, Mississippi."

"It'll be enough," Duke said.

Ripcord's expression remained skeptical.

Duke outlined a route for the truck and told Westen to wait five minutes, and then take off.

When Duke, Rip, and Stearns were alone, and close to the edge of the forest again, Rip asked, "Really think we can pull this one off, bro?"

"Yeah," Duke said. "Why not? There's three of us and only a hundred of them."

Rip accepted that as decent odds, but added, "They do have choppers and tanks."

Shrugging, Duke said, "And we've got rockets."

"They'll call for reinforcements, and shut down the borders."

"We have surprise on our side."

Rip shook his head. "You got that right—this surprises the hell out of me."

"I'm on top of it," Duke said. "That's why I'm the hero and you're the sidekick."

Rip might have been slapped. "*You're* the hero?"

he blurted, his voice rising. "In the movie in your *mind* maybe. Sidekick my achin' backside. . . ."

Grabbing the rocket launcher from Stearns, Ripcord prepared it for firing. Stearns started to protest but Duke shook his head, and Stearns backed down. Among Duke's skills as a leader was his ability to motivate his men, especially one Ripcord Weems. All he had to do was question Rip's self-image, and it was on. Whoever was in front of them, in this case the Uzekurkis, was screwed.

The only question now was the timing.

Ripcord settled in at the edge of the woods, the rocket launcher aimed squarely at the complex. Duke glanced to his left and saw the truck following the path back toward the road to the complex. When the party started, Bergman would take off cross-country and make the proverbial run for the border. . . .

From above them came the sound of helicopters still searching the woods around the complex, vainly seeking Duke's team. He hoped they would buzz home in a moment, concerned worker bees back to the hive to check on an injured queen. If they didn't, and went after the truck, the mission would fail . . . and Duke and his team would sure as hell all end up dead.

Still, he felt the plan was viable and the risk minimal. After all, these were Uzekurkis, and their long suit was following orders, not improvising. He was sure that by the time the enemy soldiers figured out what was happening, the truck would have a significant head start.

A satellite dish and an array of antennas were clearly visible atop a nearby section of the complex's roof. That would be the first target.

Using his binoculars, Duke focused on the truck and could see Westen in the passenger seat of the cab. The doc wore the uniform of the Uzekurki junior officer, who had headed the firing squad. Beyond him, also in an ill-fitting Uzekurki uniform, Bergman drove. Even through the binoculars, they both looked pretty scared. . . .

Into his com link, Duke said, "Stay calm."

"Easier said than done," Westen replied.

Duke lowered the binoculars and glanced at Rip, who stood silently, his eye pressed to the scope of the rocket launcher.

His voice low and level, Duke said, "Do it."

Rip depressed the trigger and the rocket flew from the barrel of the launcher while a white plume of vapor erupted from the back.

"Turn *now*," Duke yelled into the com link.

The rocket whooshed out of the woods and toward the complex. In the seconds it took for the rocket to fly to its target, the truck veered to the right and shot across the snow-covered plain toward the highway that ran westward into the trees.

The rocket impacted with the satellite dish and exploded, lighting up the early morning as if it were high noon. The heat of the blast swept over Duke's face, and he might have been standing too close to a campfire—a *big* one.

The shock wave rocked him backward, and then they were moving—he, Rip, and Stearns—running like hell from the position where they'd fired the rocket.

And the helicopters did just as Duke had predicted: They turned back for the complex, the two on the north converging on the spot where the team had just been.

In the complex, a claxon alarm sounded—the Uzekurkis would be on their butts right away.

"Run like hell!" Duke said into the com link.

The truck had made it across the plain, and bounced over a ditch, before rumbling up onto the westward road.

Unfortunately, a helicopter saw this, and as it turned to race after the truck, Duke yelled, *"Rip!"*

Reading his commander's mind, Ripcord and Stearns loaded another rocket into the launcher and swung their aim up at the chopper chasing after the truck.

The searchlight on the chopper was still visible as it centered on the vehicle. Just as the helicopter opened fire with its machine gun, Ripcord triggered the rocket launcher.

Sailing across the sky in the pale, red early morning light, the missile plowed a course for the helicopter. At the last second, the pilot tried to avoid the missile, but it struck the tail rotor and detonated.

The chopper spun wildly out of control and crashed into the trees, bursting into a massive orange-and-gray blossom whose shrapnel petals went flying everywhere.

Bergman's voice exploded over Duke's com link. "Westen's hit! Westen's *hit*!"

"How bad?" Duke asked.

"Looks bad," Bergman said, his voice surprisingly calm after the initial shock. "He's out. Unconscious."

"Everyone else?"

"Okay, I think."

Duke turned to look, and the truck with the rest of the team was barreling into the woods, seeming almost like a mirage as it disappeared into the trees . . . and if Duke hadn't known better, he might wonder if he'd ever seen it at all.

Suddenly, a helicopter materialized to hover in front of Duke, Stearns, and Rip, and Duke had the sudden realization that they hadn't moved quickly enough.

Machine-gun rounds ripped the snow around them, and they were on the move again, scattering, keeping low as they retreated deeper into the forest. The chopper roared overhead, an angry hunter searching out its prey. It fired its machine guns occasionally and—though he couldn't see the others—Duke hoped the Uzekurkis were firing blindly, just hoping to get lucky.

After ducking beneath a fallen tree, Duke tried to catch his breath as he swiftly scanned the forest for a sign of Rip or Stearns.

"I'm okay," said a weak voice over the com link.

Relief surged through Duke. Pressing the button on his com link, he asked, "Doc?"

"Yeah, I've got a bullet in me . . . but I'll be all right."

Duke said, "It's only twenty klicks to the border. Don't stop for anything!"

"Don't worry," Westen said.

Continuing to search the woods, Duke found the chopper first, soaring over the treetops, racing toward him as if chasing something. Then, looking at the trees, Duke saw Rip running in his direction as well, sprinting ahead of the chopper but losing ground fast.

It would only be a matter of seconds before the helicopter's machine guns would tear Duke's friend to pieces.

Raising his M16, Duke sighted through the trees, trying to get a clear shot at the helicopter. The foliage was gone for the winter, but the branches were still too thick for Duke to get a clear shot. The distance was closing, and Rip didn't seem to have a chance.

Lowering his eyes from the chopper to his buddy, even through the dim light in the forest, Duke was sure he saw Rip wink, right before the runner faked left, then made a ninety-degree right turn up the hill.

Understanding now that Rip was baiting the pilot, not fleeing from him, Duke snapped his M16 to his shoulder. The chopper followed Rip, banking right, and when it leveled, there was the pilot, right in Duke's sights.

Duke didn't flinch or hesitate: Just as with the firing squad, he let out a slow breath, and squeezed the trigger.

The pilot slumped forward, and the chopper lurched to the right and downward, the rotors catching the treetops and making frosty salad out of evergreens, the copilot struggling to control the helicopter before it made one final violent pitch forward, and crashed into the snow. After a moment that felt like a lifetime, the fuel tank exploded, lighting up the forest and riddling it with burning, flying shrapnel.

Into his com link, Duke said, "Rip, you can stop running now."

The reply came from right beside him.

"I have, buddy."

"That was a hell of a dangerous thing you just did."

"That's what heroes do. Sidekicks like *you* get to take the easy shot." Then, with a shrug, Rip said, "Kidding aside, man. You had my back."

"Always."

"Suppose we have to walk home now."

Stearns came up and joined them.

"You okay?" Duke asked.

Nodding, Stearns said, "And ready to go."

"One thing left to do," Duke said.

"Air strike?" Rip asked.

"Air strike," Duke confirmed.

He used his com link to radio the coordinates to the pilots waiting just outside Uzekurki airspace.

"Roger that," the pilot said.

Within seconds, they could hear the approaching roar of jets.

"Let's get going then," Duke said.

They started off through the woods, Duke on point.

Shaking his head, Rip said, "If you hadn't killed that pilot, we could've had a helicopter to fly home."

Without turning around, Duke said, "C'mon, you baby, it's only twenty klicks to the border. It's just good exercise."

"On a treadmill in the gym, nobody shoots at me."

"Give it time."

They moved out as the sun rose behind them. They weren't too far into the forest when the sunlight was blotted out by fireballs from dozens of bombs destroying the complex.

This time no one made a smart remark. Soldiers were dying. And they were soldiers, too.

CHAPTER TWO

Yo, JOEs!

The Pit

Blue-eyed and square-jawed, General Clayton Abernathy (code name Hawk) looked the part of the prototypical American hero—which he was.

Commander of the ultrasecret international force known as G.I. JOE, Hawk had been born and raised in Denver, Colorado, before attending the United States Military Academy at West Point, New York, where he graduated with high honors.

From there, the newly commissioned lieutenant rose quickly within the ranks of the United States Army, earning a reputation as a physically topflight fighting man, and a military strategist of considerable intellect and skill. He had become a legend as a member of the NATO forward command in Afghanistan, and as a colonel, had joined G.I. JOE as a field commander; since then, he had risen through these ranks as swiftly as he had the U.S. Army and NATO.

Now, he ran the whole show from the Pit, the subterranean command post of G.I. JOE, located in the middle of the Sahara desert, far southwest of the pyramids at Giza. The Pit served as home, high-tech armory, watch-post, and training center for the select members of the G.I. JOE team.

The top level contained a landing area for aircraft, an entrance for wheeled vehicles, and, taking up most of the space, a garage and hangar for the various G.I. JOE vehicles. Level two held a massive urban-combat training level—a sort of Hogan's Alley on steroids; the FBI's 3-D training ground *was* an alley by comparison, with the full-sized city on level two of the Pit. Level three was a Sea World-like maze of tanks used for deep-water combat training.

The fourth level held the Control Room of the Pit. This floor was no doubt the inspiration for the center's name, a huge circular chamber, half-bordered with workstations where countless smaller monitors echoed larger nearby wall-mounted flat screens. The gray marble floor and a bluish sloping ceiling were offset by the green-hued wall monitors, and a dome light illuminated a central, circular workstation where the general could display maps or charts.

The rest of the chamber was arrayed with slightly smaller wall monitors and an elevated observation post, hemmed by a cross-hatching of metal railing. The real work was going on opposite this post, technicians bent over their stations while the array of monitors, large and small, constantly shifted images and information.

Hawk's workstation was home to a vast computer/communication system, the monitor set into the tabletop; a low-tech stack of file folders perched near the general's right elbow.

Across the circular workstation from Hawk, his personal assistant, Courtney Krieger (code name Cover Girl), stood with her tablet-sized computer in one hand, so she would be free to type with the other. Slender, willowy, her legs impossibly long, Cover Girl wore her long blonde hair in a tight bun. Her big green eyes swept over whatever was on her computer screen as Hawk's remained glued to the tabletop monitor.

The streaming video originated from an American satellite over Uzekurkistan. Hawk was watching a line of trucks pulling out of a circular complex that sat in the middle of a plain.

"How old is this footage?" he asked.

"Not quite six hours," Cover Girl said.

As the G.I. JOE commander watched now, the leader of the insertion team shot down a helicopter. Hawk had already been impressed with the way he had kept his cool when the mission seemed about to go sideways. Something had happened to alert the Uzekurkis to the insertion team's presence before the satellite got into position for the general to watch the rest of the action unfold.

Hawk asked, "What did you say the team leader's name was?"

Cover Girl touched a button on the small hand-held computer. "Hauser, sir," she said. "Conrad S."

"And what do we know about him?"

Very little got to Hawk without first going through Cover Girl. Born in Peoria, Illinois, and having given up a successful modeling career, Krieger had joined the Army wanting to serve her country . . . and to prove she was more than just a pretty face.

While in the service, she earned a master's degree in political science; this was a young woman with a clear understanding of world politics, and of what was really important as opposed to what, at any given moment, merely *seemed* important.

After excelling in the Army, Krieger had been recruited to join G.I. JOE. Her training exemplary, she had proven herself an excellent field agent as well. Battle wounds had led her to the position of Hawk's aide-de-camp, and she was one of the few noncombatants in the program.

Cover Girl touched several buttons on the computer-tablet, then said, "Born in St. Louis, Missouri, Hauser spoke two languages when he enlisted, and learned Chinese and several other Asian dialects at the Army's Special Languages School. He graduated at the top of his class in Airborne school at Fort Benning. He spent time with Special Forces in Asia before teaching at several Special Forces schools. His nickname is Duke."

"Did he get those scientists out alive?"

"Every single one, sir," Cover Girl said. "They crossed the border, got picked up by an Army helicopter, and have now been flown to the military hospital at Ramstein Air Force Base for checkups and debriefing."

"Any casualties?"

"Sir, the insertion team's medical officer was gravely wounded when a helicopter strafed the escape vehicle."

"No one else?"

Cover Girl shook her head. "Not so much as a scratch, sir."

The general lifted an eyebrow, which indicated he was particularly impressed. "Cover Girl, we'll want to keep an eye on Lieutenant Hauser."

"Yes, General."

"Might even be G.I. JOE material."

"I'll make a note, sir."

The general waved a finger at the wall monitor. "Is that his XO, who led the chopper to him?"

"Yes, sir."

"And his name . . . ?"

"Wallace Weems, sir. Ripcord to his friends and fellow soldiers."

"Bio?"

"Expert marksman, second only to Duke within their battalion, weapons specialist, and . . . I think you'll find this of particular interest . . . he's qualified in jets."

"Jets?" Hawk asked, with a mild frown. "He's a pilot, but stays mostly on the ground?"

"That's what his file says," Cover Girl said.

Hawk nodded thoughtfully. "I want to keep an eye on *him,* too."

"Yes, sir."

Hawk was not the be-all and end-all when it came to choosing who became members of G.I. JOE and who didn't but his opinion carried more weight than most. He always had a few soldiers worldwide on whom he was keeping tabs, as possible members.

"Ripcord would appear rash," Hawk said. "But

with a little training and seasoning, he might be G.I. JOE material himself."

"Yes, sir," Cover Girl said. "They do seem to be something of a team, Hauser and Weems."

"That has its positives."

"And its negatives, sir."

"And its negatives," Hawk allowed.

No matter who they were, Duke, Ripcord, or anyone else for that matter, sooner or later they would have to be cleared by Hawk, just as had nearly everyone in the pile of folders perched on the corner of his workstation.

That he felt more comfortable with physical file folders and documents than strictly computer-provided information probably said something about his age, Hawk supposed. That he was old-school, and something of a dinosaur, in this high-tech world was not lost on him.

Hawk asked, "What of the weapons?"

"Assuming they were in the trucks," Cover Girl said, "they are now in the wind."

Hawk nodded. "Not entirely, of course."

Cover Girl looked slightly confused. "Really?"

Tapping the stack of files on his desk, Hawk said, "I know *where* the weapons are headed . . . and Unit Alpha will be there to meet them when they arrive."

"You *know* where the weapons are going?"

"We have pretty good intel on this," Hawk said, switching off the monitor on the wall.

Of course, this whole matter would have been much easier if Duke's team had just destroyed the weapons before they left the complex; but Hawk

a) knew that that wasn't Lieutenant Hauser's mission; and b) he also doubted that Hauser even knew that the damn things were there.

Hawk, through his connections with the Army, was well aware of the details of the mission . . . and also that the safe return of the scientists was the Army's only concern. Traditional military tended to be of the moment; G.I. JOE took a longer view.

"So," Cover Girl asked, "what's their final destination?"

Hawk summoned a world map on his tabletop monitor, and touched South America, filling the screen with it.

"There," he said.

Cover Girl stared at the continent. "That represents quite a few places where those weapons could wind up . . . and do a lot of harm."

"No argument," Hawk said with a nod.

"Do you know exactly where those weapons are headed?"

"I can make a more-than-educated guess, Cover Girl . . . and so can you."

She studied the map. "The major countries are all stable, at least for the most part."

"Agreed," Hawk said.

"That leaves the minor countries."

"How many of those seem unstable to you?"

His aide's eyes wandered from country to country. "Any number. But there's a standout—the strongest of the possibilities. . . ."

"Which is?"

She took her time.

Finally, she said, "San Sebastiao."

His smile was a thin, wide line. "Correct. Now . . . tell me what you think about this situation."

Again, Cover Girl gathered her thoughts, then locked eyes with the general. "That's what makes this more an educated guess than a certainty."

"What is?"

"Something about it doesn't make sense. If you don't mind my saying so, sir."

"Not at all. But what doesn't make sense to you?"

She frowned and it did nothing to diminish her modelesque beauty. "The rebels in San Sebastiao could *never* afford weapons like these."

He tented his fingers. "Go on."

"President Vicente has always been friendly to the U.S., and—although his country's vast oil reserves give him plenty of money to afford these weapons—he's never shown any sign of being brutal, or vindictive, against the rebels. He's always tried to maintain the peace . . . so why buy next-generation weapons from . . . uh, who exactly *is* he buying them from?"

Hawk shook his head. "We still haven't tracked down the salesman, or for that matter who's buying them. But your assessment is typically spot-on. If the rebels can't afford them, and Vicente wouldn't buy them . . . then who is?"

Cover Girl had no answer for that. "What now, then?"

"Now, I go back to choosing who will represent us in San Sebastiao," Hawk said. "And you start making the logistical plan."

"Yes, sir," Cover Girl said.

Hawk picked up his files and made for his stateroom office, a modest-sized, spartanly furnished room decorated with framed diplomas, awards, and photographs taken throughout a distinguished career, highlighted not by the most impressive individuals he'd encountered but the bravest of fighting men and women.

Alone with his stack of files, Hawk ran a hand through his hair and let out a long breath. He was tired. G.I. JOE had been putting out more than its fair share of fires around the world lately.

He had the gut feeling that there was something happening on a deeper, more subtle level than merely the usual political upheavals that took place—possibly something global.

Still, it was just a feeling. So far, at least, he had no proof, not even any clues—just that thing gnawing at his gut that something not *normal* was going on.

Had he been working too long, and too hard, without a break? Was it compromising his judgment?

No, he told himself. But he couldn't shake the feeling that he had seen a ghost. . . .

Hawk picked up the first file from the top of the heap and silently read the name: *Ettienne R. LaFitte—Code Name: Gung Ho.*

Tall, muscular, with clipped brown hair, blue eyes, and a hard-set jaw, Gung Ho specialized in recon and jungle warfare. Born to a Cajun clan in Fer-de-Lance, Louisiana, Gung Ho had moved to New Orleans, where he earned a reputation as both a bare-knuckle brawler and knife fighter.

At eighteen, Gung Ho joined the United States Marine Corps, graduating with top honors from boot camp at Parris Island. After airborne, recon, and ordnance schools, he distinguished himself in the Corps, coming to the attention of G.I. JOE. He joined early on, and had been a major part of the team ever since.

Hawk had already decided on Gung Ho to lead Unit Alpha on this particular sortie. Rereading the file, Hawk found himself returning to one of the missions that had brought Gung Ho to the attention of G.I. JOE. In fact, Gung Ho had been leading a team not unlike the one Duke Hauser had led in Uzekurkistan today.

As part of the United States' war on drugs, Gung Ho's insertion team dropped into a nameless South American jungle to destroy a major cocaine manufacturing facility. The jungle was thick with undergrowth in the valley, the sun beating down relentlessly, the ten-man insertion team having come far enough to sweat-soak every inch of their camouflage uniforms as they labored through the foliage, careful to look for trip wires and tiger-pit traps along the way, not to mention the occasional poisonous snake.

The team was still a good ten klicks from the objective when machine-gun fire erupted all around them.

Two of Gung Ho's men went down, and the rest dove, finding cover wherever they could. Pinned by two machine-gun nests, the team seemed powerless to fight back. The two nests were fifty yards ahead, one to the left, one to the right, catching the insertion team in a lethal cross fire.

Gung Ho rose and took off to his right, sprinting serpentine through the jungle, screaming as he went, drawing the fire of both enemy positions. Around him, leaves blew to vapor and tree trunks splintered to kindling as round after round pounded.

Still, lungs burning, Gung Ho kept moving.

Behind him, his team was able to start returning fire, and the withering fusillade aimed at Gung Ho somewhat abated.

Circling around, Gung Ho came up behind the five men in the machine-gun nest on the right, and emptied the clip of his M16 their way, then lobbed a hand grenade as a cherry on the lethal sundae. The primary weapon and every other gun in the nest turned in Gung Ho's direction, and started blasting with no regard for any of their comrades who might still be drawing breath.

Hightailing it out, Gung Ho used the cover fire from his team to circle back into the jungle. Two bad guys from the surviving machine-gun nest took off after him—both wearing green camouflage, one tall, one short.

The tall guy came rushing past a tree and was met by the butt of Gung Ho's M16. He went down in a heap without so much as a murmur of protest. The short one got off a shot into the air before the blade of Gung Ho's knife ripped out his throat from behind.

Doubling back to the machine-gun nest, Gung Ho found the other three shooters had returned their attention to his team, trying to mow them down.

One enemy heard Gung Ho coming, turned, and got a knife flung at him, the blade arcing end over end before burying itself in the man's chest. He was dead before he went down.

A second one turned, AK–47 in hand.

Gung Ho kicked the gun out of the man's grasp, and chopped him in the throat with a knife-edge strike. As the man grabbed at his neck, Gung Ho's palm drove the man's nose bone through his brain, a relatively quick and merciful death. As the body crumpled, Gung Ho stepped over it, and—before the last man could turn—Gung Ho snapped his neck.

In the end, bad intelligence had been at fault.

The manufacturing facility had been moved, the machine-gun nests left behind as a welcoming committee for whoever came snooping around.

If Gung Ho's actions had occurred during a recognized war, he might have won the Medal of Honor. Since it went down in a South American jungle, in a battle no one was supposed to know about, all the valiant soldier had earned was a promotion . . . but that promotion had been to G.I. JOE.

Now, he was one of Hawk's best team leaders.

Yes, Gung Ho would definitely be the honcho of Unit Alpha when they went to South America, where his previous experience would be a plus.

Setting the file aside, Hawk picked up the next one. This, too, was an obvious choice for Unit Alpha—Snake Eyes.

Despite being mute, the silent, extremely lethal

Snake Eyes had become a fixture within G.I. JOE. An expert with small arms, katana, throwing stars, and knives, and hand-to-hand combat instructor for all of G.I. JOE, Snake Eyes was himself as much weapon as he was human.

Always dressed from head to toe in black, including a ninja hood, a sleek visor providing him vision, the block red symbol of the Arashikage Clan adorning his right shoulder, Snake Eyes—despite the violence of which he was capable—sought peace, both inwardly and outwardly. Lonzo Wilkinson (code name Stalker)—one of the first to join G.I. JOE—had recruited Snake Eyes after the two had served together in the U.S. Army Rangers.

Hawk never failed to marvel at the courage, resourcefulness, and lethal skills of G.I. JOE's resident ninja. These qualities had all been underlined on a recent, highly volatile mission, when Snake Eyes had been sent to free some diplomats held by terrorists inside an embassy in a West African nation.

The ninja had gotten to the three-story marble building by hang gliding onto the roof. From there, he entered through a ventilation shaft, coming out in a vacant office on the top floor. Next, he crept to a corner office, where he found a gunman watching out the window.

The first and last sound the sniper heard was the *whoosh* of air from Snake Eyes's katana just before it severed his head. The second sniper in the next corner office realized he wasn't alone perhaps a second sooner than his comrade had. The man had almost turned around when the long sword pierced his heart.

Two more snipers on that floor fell under the steel of Snake Eyes's katana. Six on the second floor dropped under a combination of knives and throwing stars. The final eight on the first floor—the ones holding the hostages—all died silently, each taken out by the ninja's martial arts talents.

The diplomats all walked out unharmed.

Snake Eyes, though a loner by nature, did have a few close friends, and had even developed a special friendship with fellow G.I. JOE team member Shana O'Hara. The reasons for their bond were unclear and largely unknown to General Hawk, though perhaps the female's cool-headed, unemotional approach was one with which the ninja could identify.

And in fact the next file Hawk selected was O'Hara's. Five eight, with a trim frame both shapely and muscular, Shana O'Hara (code name Scarlett) had been the first woman recruited to G.I. JOE.

The lovely redhead came from a family of martial arts instructors, and had begun her own martial arts training at nine, earning a black belt in Tae Kwon Do by fifteen. In addition to her hand-to-hand combat skills, Scarlett also mastered the crossbow, a weapon she still favored in her G.I. JOE assignments.

Scarlett and Snake Eyes worked so well together, it was as if Hawk were sending three soldiers, not two—total professionals, and consummate teammates.

This had been borne out many times, though Hawk recalled what was perhaps the pair's most memorable adventure together. . . .

On a rescue mission in the desert, Snake Eyes and Scarlett had been separated from their team members, and set upon not by enemy troops but sword-wielding nomads. Surrounded, the two fought side by side, back-to-back, with Scarlett at one point vaulting over Snake Eyes to deliver a kick to the face of a particularly persistent foe.

After dispatching the dozen nomads, the duo had finally run into actual enemy soldiers, and taken out another dozen, about evenly divided between the ninja's sword wounds and the amazon's crossbow bolts.

General Hawk's smile was thin, and his eyes were narrowed, as he felt a quiet wave of confidence come over him. With the three-pronged leadership of Gung Ho, Snake Eyes, and Scarlett, Hawk had a beating heart for Unit Alpha on this particular mission. Now, he need only add some real firepower. . . .

And that meant Hershel Dalton, an African-American classical guitarist who could not only make a six-string sing, but who had the same ability with a Man-Portable Heavy Weapons System— basically a handheld Gatling gun too heavy for most men to lift.

Over six feet and weighing in at a muscular two-twenty, Dalton (code name Heavy Duty) had black hair cropped to the scalp, large brown eyes, and a quiet disposition, which some mistook for indifference. Hawk, however, found Heavy Duty anything *but* indifferent—thoughtful, yes; indifferent, no way. . . .

The team was pretty much complete now, except for a communications expert, and for this, inevitably, Hawk chose Breaker.

A Frenchman of Arabic descent, this somewhat diminutive communications expert spoke seven languages and had better toys to play with than any communications officer in any army in the world. His combat experience could not compare to the others on the team, but the man was as brave as he was smart, and he was *very* smart. . . .

With his team selected, the general pressed a button on his intercom and got an immediate response.

Cover Girl said, "Yes, sir?"

"Time to go to work," Hawk said.

Seconds later, Cover Girl entered his office, her computer-tablet at the ready. "Sir?"

Hawk handed her the files for the team he had chosen for this mission. "Gather them up, and have them in the conference room in fifteen minutes."

"Yes, sir—anything else, sir?"

"Are the briefing materials ready?"

"Yes, sir, everything is set with the presentation. The room's ready when you are."

"Thanks, Cover Girl."

Fifteen minutes later, Hawk strode in and, wall screen to his back, said, "At ease." Unit Alpha took the nearest conference-table chairs—Gung Ho closest, Heavy Duty opposite, leaning back. Next to him sat Snake Eyes and Scarlett, with Breaker across the way. All of their attention was on their commander.

Hawk said, "The United States is preparing a mission to San Sebastiao."

Their faces betrayed no reaction, though this meant they would be going to one of the world's most dangerous hot spots.

"Gung Ho," Hawk said, "brief us on San Sebastiao."

"Tiny country wedged among Brazil, Colombia, and Venezuela. Lots of oil." He twitched a smile. "Lots of money."

"All right," Hawk said. "Scarlett—politics?"

As if reading from a prepared and well-memorized script, Scarlett said, "President Vicente was just elected to his second term. The country is a democracy, but they are having trouble with rebels, who are pushing a socialist agenda and want to nationalize the oil. So far, the military has been up to the challenge, though the army's commander, General Pedro Lopez, is rumored to have his eye on the president's chair as well."

"Let's keep *our* eyes on General Lopez." Hawk said. "But there is a new wrinkle of which few are aware."

Eyes tightened.

Hawk said, "One of the players in the San Sebastiao mess has decided to buy some next-generation weapons, in order to tilt the table in their favor."

The team listened intently without interruption.

"We don't know who's buying, who's selling, or who's going to end up with them," Hawk said. "We just know that the weapons are headed for

San Sebastiao, and that the Americans are sending a team in to stop them."

Heavy Duty asked, "Then why send *us* in?"

Hawk bestowed half a smile on the big man. "Good question, Heavy D. Let me answer it with a question. Who has better intel than G.I. JOE?"

"No one," he said.

"And what do *we* know?" Hawk asked.

"Sounds like," Gung Ho said, "pretty much bupkus, sir."

Nodding, Hawk said, "We're the best and we know barely a damn thing. What do you suppose the Americans know?"

An uncomfortable silence settled over the room, but Scarlett broke it: "I would say even less than us, sir."

"Roger that." Hawk's eyes went to Heavy Duty. "And that's why we're sending you in. The world can't know our part in this. The Americans will get the credit for stopping this threat, after *we* stop it . . . but that's the way it has to be."

No one expressed the rationale, but all knew it: For G.I. JOE to function properly, they must operate in the shadows, virtually nonexistent.

"So," Hawk continued, "your mission is to stop these weapons from falling into the hands of the different factions and, equally important, make it look as though the *American* team was solely responsible."

Breaker asked, "How are we supposed to do that, sir?"

"Well, if the American team is up to the task, let them handle it. I've been gathering data on the team leader, and he's damned good." He shook his head. "Still, my guess is that they'll be in over their heads on this one. You will supply support for the U.S. team."

Breaker asked, "Are we glorified babysitters on this one, sir?"

Hawk took no offense at the question. "If so, the Americans are tough babies. But they're up against adversaries who would be a challenge to any insertion team—including the one in this room. Understood?"

"Yes, sir," they said in unison.

"Back them up without their knowledge," Hawk said.

"No problem," Heavy Duty said with just a touch of sarcasm.

Hawk gave him a hard look.

"Sir," Heavy Duty said cheerfully. "No problem, sir!"

"Good," Hawk said. His chin hiked an inch. "Stop the weapons from being delivered. Destroy them. And make sure that under no circumstances do you interact with the U.S. team. Understood?"

"Yes, *sir*," they said in unison.

"Now," Hawk said. "Pack up and get ready to move. Yo, JOEs!"

As one, they rose and yelled, "Yo, JOEs!"

Hawk was, as usual, heartened by their camaraderie.

They would need it.

CHAPTER THREE
Barbaric Notions

San Sebastiao

President Martin Vicente certainly did not consider himself royalty; nonetheless, he was royally ticked off.

Barely into his second term, Vicente knew he didn't have the luxury of anger, however, and he was using these few moments alone in his office as a sort of time-out.

In his fifties, his hair still jet-black if receding rapidly, Vicente was showing the rigors of his office in more than five years of working to make San Sebastiao a better place for its citizens. Pouches had filled under his eyes, wrinkles had formed at the corners of his mouth, and crow's-feet sprouted around his eyes. An ulcer ate away at his stomach, and he slept only a couple of hours every night. Today, he wore a charcoal-gray suit with a light blue shirt and a dark tie with a light blue geometric design—his favorite tie, a Christmas gift from his oldest daughter, Maria.

The office in which he sat was more elegant than Vicente might have preferred—the wide desk polished mahogany and clear of any clutter other than a telephone, a photo of his wife and two lovely girls, and the file he had just been reading. Across the desk were two brown leather chairs with a round mahogany table between. Paintings of San Sebastiaoan presidents and generals watched him from three walls, with the other given over to a huge window overlooking the expansive, beautifully tended lawn of the presidential palace. Longer than it was wide, the office had a sitting area at the far end with four wing chairs on the corners of a coffee table, a sofa on either of two long sides—comfortable seating for at least eight.

The whole place felt too prestigious, too antiseptic for Vicente's tastes. He was a working president, not some figurehead, and would have felt more at home in a small office with a messy desk littered with files, just as he'd had when he was an attorney working to overcome the corrupt government of the preceding administration.

Now, with the corruption weeded out (at least for the most part), Vicente could see the democracy of his dreams glimmering on the horizon. Still, there was much left to do and time was running out—between the rebels trying to overthrow the government, and the prospect of a difficult third-term election less than three years away, Vicente felt that he was trying to save his country from a ticking bomb that would explode at some undetermined moment. . . .

Today, he still had the meeting with Lopez and Chernitz; then he was to meet with the leadership of the national assembly at the Capitol Building.

Rubbing a hand over his face, trying fruitlessly to fend off exhaustion, Vicente let out a long breath, then slipped his glasses back on and returned to the file on his desk.

It contained a report from General Pedro Lopez. Although Lopez had been a member of the previous administration, Vicente had kept him on as head of San Sebastiao's military; the general was popular with the citizens, and had achieved an outstanding record of service.

Though a man of peace, Vicente had read and even studied *The Art Of War,* ancient Chinese general Sun-tzu's book on military strategy, which advised: "Keep your friends close, and your enemies closer." That thought summed up exactly why Vicente had kept Lopez in his position. The general had done nothing to openly subvert Vicente's administration, yet the president's mistrust for the man ran deep enough for Vicente to keep Lopez not just close, but on a very short leash.

Lopez's report concerned intelligence indicating that the rebels were in the market to purchase next-generation weapons from an eastern European arms dealer. The general, who had an acquaintanceship with arms dealer Emile Chernitz, suggested that Chernitz might be persuaded to sell the weapons to the government instead—*if* the price was right.

Such deals with devils were distasteful to Vincente; but for the well-being of his country, he had to at least consider this one. Which was why he was prepping for the upcoming meeting, and even *thinking* about speaking to a *pendejo* gunrunner like Chernitz.

Vicente set the report aside and picked up a blue-print of the next-generation pulse rifle that Chernitz was peddling. The theory behind the pulse rifle was that it used a capacitor-discharge bank and inductive coil to produce rapid magneto-inductive pulses that would both accelerate the projectile and make the weapon's aim even truer. Each nonmagnetic shell contained a small explosive charge so that even if the shooter did miss, if the shot was close enough, the explosive could still lead to a kill shot.

This was the sort of weapon that could change the outcome of a battle, or even (Vicente knew) a revolution. Everything he stood for warned against going down this path. There was no moral ground for buying weapons like these from a black market dealer, especially when Vicente knew they would be used against citizens of San Sebastiao—even if they were citizens trying to violently overthrow him.

A man had to stand for something, didn't he?

Yet even with his *"Voz de mi alma,"* as he called it, *the voice of my soul,* warning him against such an action, Vicente was still pragmatic enough to look at the situation from the other side. Weapons like this could quell a revolution quickly, and—though it would cost the lives of San Sebastiaoan rebels—how many innocent lives would the weapons save?

He would consider the counsel of his vice president, Jose Ansalmo; but the president was fairly sure he already knew what decision he was going to make. Vicente wondered if history would remember him as a man of conviction, who did the right thing . . . or would he be seen as a coward, who wouldn't do what was necessary to protect his country?

A knock came at the office door.

"*Entre,*" Vicente said, closing the file and slipping it into a drawer.

A tall, broad-shouldered man entered; he wore a gray pinstripe suit with a white shirt and gray tie with red and blue stripes, and exuded confidence and professionalism.

"*Señor Presidente,*" he said.

"Come in, Jose," Vicente said, gesturing to a leather chair opposite.

Vice President Jose Ansalmo strode to the president's desk. In his late forties, his full head of hair still black, swept back, Ansalmo bore piercing brown eyes, a concrete jaw, and a neatly trimmed goatee.

"*Gracias, Señor Presidente,*" Ansalmo said, and sat.

Forgoing the pleasantries, Vicente asked, "What do you make of this . . . this *thing* that Lopez has brought to us?"

Taking his time, getting his thoughts in order, Ansalmo met the president's gaze.

This was a quality Vicente respected about his vice president. The man never spoke until he really had something to say.

"*Señor Presidente,*" Ansalmo said, "I hope you are not giving serious consideration to this scheme of Lopez's."

"I have no choice, Jose," Vicente said.

Ansalmo's eyes flashed. "No choice but to—"

"To give it consideration. Serious consideration."

The vice president began to protest, but Vicente
stopped him with an upraised palm.

"I must seriously consider anything that will
save this country from rebellion," the president
said, "just as you would, were you sitting in this
chair. But, like you, Jose"—he sighed—"I find the
whole matter repugnant, and I have no desire to
bring such weapons into our country, any more
than you."

A tiny smile played at the corners of Ansalmo's
mouth. "I am happy to hear you say that, *Señor
Presidente.*"

"The question now is . . . how do we keep this
dog Chernitz from selling the weapons to the
rebels?"

Ansalmo shook his head. "That, *Señor Presidente,* I do not know."

They both considered the situation for a long moment. Unlike lawyer Vicente—who had, more or less,
been forced into politics by the corruption he saw
around him—Ansalmo had been a lifelong politi-
cian. He'd started as a provincial representative in
the national assembly, then worked as a senator
within the same assembly, until Vicente recognized
a kindred spirit and asked Ansalmo to become his
vice president.

Ansalmo sat forward. "Perhaps we might approach the Americans . . . ?"

Vicente regarded the option. He wondered if the

United States government would even consider getting involved with the sale of weapons. Although the American president had up till now seemed empathetic to San Sebastiao's problems, any aid had been strictly of the financial variety; no political help within the United Nations had been forthcoming, either, no arms, no soldiers, and—although American money was always welcome—with San Sebastiao's oil income, money was the least of the small nation's problems.

Ansalmo offered, "Perhaps the Americans could exert pressure on Chernitz."

Shaking his head, Vicente said, "I doubt they will want to get so directly involved . . . but I will bring it up to Ambassador Nolan, when I see him tomorrow."

Nodding, Ansalmo said, "Explain that this might be their final opportunity to keep such weapons off the continent, and out of the hemisphere."

"I agree," Vicente said, nodding back. "We have to try to involve the Americans in this, or our country may well pay a price far more dear than the merely monetary."

"Let me pose another question," Ansalmo said, his voice lower now, more conspiratorial.

"You can ask me anything, Jose—you know that."

The vice president glanced around the room, as if someone—or something—might be eavesdropping; then he leaned forward and asked, "Where do you think General Lopez stands on this issue?"

The question surprised Vicente. "He wants the

weapons, of course! He's a military man, Jose—they *always* want the weapons. Lopez was, after all, the one who suggested this meeting."

"I wasn't talking about his desire for the weapons," Ansalmo said. "He lusts for power as if it were a beautiful woman."

Vincente frowned in thought. "Then why the question?"

"I refer not to where he stands on the weapons, *Señor Presidente* . . . rather, on Chernitz. Is the general's alliance to us, or to the gunrunner?"

Vicente shifted in his leather chair. "If you mean, do I think General Lopez is receiving a kickback on the sale of these weapons, I would be astonished if he were not."

Ansalmo gave a slight shake of his head. "I do not doubt his venality. I refer instead to his loyalty—is he more loyal to Chernitz than he is to his country?"

The president considered this for a long moment, though this notion was no stranger to him. "Admittedly, I sometimes look for the best in people . . . even the ones who might not deserve it. Still, I do not believe that Lopez would choose money over country."

"Señor Presidente," Ansalmo said, "I hope you are correct, but I am not worried about General Lopez picking money over San Sebastiao. In fact, my concern is exactly the opposite. I am afraid he might choose San Sebastiao."

Vicente discerned Ansalmo's meaning; but the thought was so unfathomable that he had pushed it from his mind.

"Do not mince words, Jose," the president said. "Tell me in the frankest terms what you are thinking."

Rising, Ansalmo said, "General Lopez has us painted into a corner, my friend. If we buy the weapons, Lopez's army ends up with them . . . and after he deals with the rebels, what's to stop him from turning these pulse weapons on us? If we do not buy these arms, then we have to guard that Lopez does not assassinate us, and make the deal with Chernitz after we're gone."

Vincente's expression was grave; so was his tone: "You think these are the only two possible outcomes, after this meeting today?"

"I suppose Lopez might make the deal, and *then* assassinate us." Ansalmo shrugged. "In any case, Lopez has cast his lot with the gunrunner, and together they may well use these weapons to destroy the democracy of San Sebastiao . . . and turn it into the general's own private dictatorship."

With a brief nod, Vicente said, "That thought had occurred to me. Do you really think the general is capable of such treason?"

"Oh, yes, *Señor Presidente*, I do. That does not mean he *will* do it . . . but underestimating the greed of others is a good way to find yourself dead, when you are in our position."

Vicente opened a desk drawer and withdrew a pack of American cigarettes, a lighter, and a glass ashtray; he shook a cigarette out, then offered one to Ansalmo, who declined. Replacing the pack in the desk, Vicente fired up the cigarette—he had stopped smoking years ago, but in times of crisis, such as this, he would allow himself a lapse.

Vicente drew a long drag as he considered his options. He blew the smoke out through his nostrils, enjoying his first cigarette in nearly a year. He had considered the possibility of assassination since he first thought about running for office. He knew the chance existed.

Perhaps surprisingly, his first thought was not for himself, but for his family, and only then his country. Vicente did not think of himself as the only one who could lead San Sebastiao.

In fact, he had chosen Jose Ansalmo as his vice president because he considered the man even better-suited for leading the country than himself. No, his concern for his nation, already in deep political turmoil, was that an assassination might sink San Sebastiao into full-scale civil war. That kind of violence could set them back decades, and cost thousands of lives.

"If that happens," Vincente said, "if Lopez is a treasonous pig, and he kills me? Then it will be up to you, Jose, to lead this country, and to keep Lopez from taking power."

Ansalmo nodded. "My first priority is to keep you alive, *Señor Presidente*."

"I'll worry about that, Jose, and keeping *you* alive as well . . . but your first priority will be the country, this you must promise me. San Sebastiao is more important than either of us, and certainly more important than General Lopez."

The vice president locked eyes with Vicente.

"*Señor Presidente,* you have my word. The country will come first."

Vicente stubbed out the cigarette in the ashtray. "We've worked too hard, for too long, to allow Lopez, or anyone else, to destroy our democracy."

"*Sí, Señor Presidente.*"

With a quick nod, Vicente pushed a button on his intercom. "Send them in."

Vicente and Ansalmo moved to the office's sitting area and took positions near the door as it opened, and two men entered.

First through the door was General Pedro Lopez, a shade less than six feet, his tan uniform adorned with all manner of colorful stripes, epaulets, and medals. His officer's cap had snippets of black visor visible through gold braids, with the country's national crest framed in red on the front.

Despite being nearly sixty, Lopez had jet-black hair, thanks less to good genes and more to a strict dye regimen. His skin was only a shade darker than his uniform, his eyes a very dark brown, and he carried himself with the erect bearing of a lifelong military man.

The general shook hands first with Ansalmo, then with Vicente, giving the president a firm, show-off's grip. Stepping to one side, he said, "*Señor Presidente,* allow me to present Mr. Emile Chernitz."

Taller and younger than Lopez, Chernitz appeared to be in his mid-forties, with swept-back brown hair and a salt-and-pepper beard. His cold eyes were like dark seeds stuck in the dough of his pasty complexion; this, Vincente thought, was surely a man who spent ninety-nine percent of his time indoors.

When Chernitz shook Vicente's hand, the arms dealer's skin felt clammy, with no strength in his grip whatsoever. To Vicente, he might have been shaking hands with a cadaver—the only difference was the man's false smile, which displayed two rows of evenly spaced teeth turned yellow by either coffee or tobacco, or both.

"A pleasure to meet you, Mr. President," Chernitz said, just a trace of his European background in his voice.

The four men took seats, Vicente and Ansalmo on the two sofas, Chernitz and Lopez in wing chairs.

"Mr. President," Chernitz said, "have you had a chance to examine General Lopez's report?"

"Yes," Vicente said, his voice icy.

The arms dealer said, "If you would like, we can set up a test firing for you, so you can see what these magnificent weapons can do in a real-world setting."

Shaking his head, Vicente said, "That won't be necessary."

With the confidence of a man who knew he had already won, Lopez asked, "You have already made up your mind, *Señor Presidente*?"

"*Sí,*" Vicente said, "I have."

Lopez and Chernitz sat forward with anticipation, and in this moment, Vicente's suspicions were confirmed: Lopez had indeed tied his horse to Chernitz's wagon.

Vincente's smile was faint. "We will not be buying the weapons. I do apologize for the trouble you've been put to, Mr. Chernitz, and appreciate your offer."

Chernitz and Lopez exchanged a shocked look.

"*Señor Presidente,*" Lopez said, "are you quite certain this is the course you wish to take?"

"*Sí.*"

Lopez shook his head. "With all due respect, *Señor Presidente,* you are handing the country over to the rebels."

Vincente's faint smile took on a chill. "Only if Mr. Chernitz insists on selling these weapons to the rebels. He could choose *not* to."

Chernitz smiled—he might have been a teacher given charge of a slow child. "Mr. President, the weapons have to be sold to someone. That is the nature of the beast. To put it frankly, I have to make a living."

"But," Vincente said, his tone sharp, "you don't have to make it in San Sebastiao."

Silence hung between the two men, the palpable tension like a living thing.

Turning to Ansalmo, the frustrated Lopez said, "*Señor Vice Presidente,* surely you cannot be agreeing with this madness . . . it . . . it approaches *treason.*"

Ansalmo's expression was as hard as that of the president. "Such an accusation itself might be considered near treason, General."

"Of course, I meant no disrespect—"

"I support President Vincente's decision," Ansalmo said, flatly. "Keeping weapons of this nature out of our country is *not* treason, General, it is only good sense. These weapons will bring our country death and suffering—no matter which side has them."

Lopez had nothing to say to that.

Trying one more time, his voice oozing reason, Chernitz said, "That may be true, Mr. Vice President, but the death and suffering will be less on the side that *has* the weapons. More important, they will also be the victors."

Rising, President Vicente said, "Señor Chernitz, I'm sure in your mind that that is justification enough. I, however, am responsible not just to the *winning* side, but to all the people of San Sebastiao, the rebels included. What would the people think of a government that purchased such weapons only to turn them on its own citizens?"

All of the men were on their feet now.

Lopez's voice had an angry edge. "The rebels aren't citizens."

"Certainly they are," Vicente said. "Even though they disagree with their government, even though they have taken up arms against that government, they are still citizens of this country . . . as are their families, many of whom may side with us. I must consider what is best for *all* the citizens of San Sebastiao—not just the ones who agree with our policies."

"Noble words, sir," Lopez said. "But, I'm afraid, naïve sentiments."

"Perhaps," Chernitz said, ever the hopeful salesman, "there is *another* course of action."

Vicente said nothing, but his expression said, *I'm listening. . . .*

The arms dealer continued: "I will soon have another product that may assist you . . . and one you will find less . . . distasteful."

Vincente and his vice president stood there in an uneasy silence shared with the general, who did not seem to know what Chernitz was talking about.

"Even as we speak, Mr. President," the arms dealer said, "top-flight scientists are at work in Asia. They are developing what you might call a . . . super soldier."

"*Super* soldier?" Lopez asked, obviously interested.

"Yes," Chernitz said. "Soldiers who feel no fear."

"There is no such thing," Ansalmo said, almost derisively. "I fought in the army of San Sebastiao in various border disputes with our neighbors, and I can assure you that *every* soldier who has *ever* fought in *any* battle has felt *fear* . . . unless he is deranged."

"Quite true," Chernitz said. "*Until now.* Once these experiments are completed, and the serum is developed, you will be able to field an army of super soldiers who will feel no pain. In addition, they will have body armor so nearly impenetrable that losses will be insignificant."

"How long until they're ready?" Lopez asked, barely able to contain himself.

President Vicente cut him off. "*No!* We want no part of any of this. No weapons now, no super soldiers later. You would give some Frankenstein's serum to our soldiers, so that they might act recklessly and foolishly? These are barbaric notions,

and not in keeping with the Geneva Convention."
He pointed to the door. "Mr. Chernitz, I want you
out of the country *tonight*!"

Chernitz began to make another point but Vicente raised a palm, cutting him off.

"You have our answer, *Señor,*" Vicente said,
ending the meeting.

Ansalmo showed them the door. While the arms
dealer seemed merely disappointed, the general looked
genuinely angry. He hung back until Chernitz was
beyond the closed door.

"*Señor Presidente,*" Lopez said, "I implore you
to change your mind. The history of warfare tells
us that those in control of superior weaponry will
inevitably prevail—such weapons, like the atom
bomb, are inhumane and, yes, even barbaric. But
the side who uses them *wins*. And, sir, these rebels
will destroy this country, if we let them. If they gain
access to Chernitz's arms, well . . . what then?"

Even though Lopez had addressed Vicente, it
was Ansalmo who answered: "Then, General, we
must not let them do that. Wouldn't that be the
military's job?"

Pouncing, Lopez said, "We could if we had the
proper weapons!"

"You *have* the proper weapons, General," Vicente insisted. "It's the *improper* weapons I refuse
to sanction."

Sensing the futility of his situation, Lopez said,
"*Sí, Señor Presidente.* I mean only to serve you and
my country."

Nodding, Vicente said, "Good. Now that we are
in agreement, you are dismissed."

Lopez, seething at the slight, simply said, *"Sí, Señor Presidente."* He snapped a salute, then retreated to the door, which Ansalmo closed behind him.

"You were not easy on him," Ansalmo said. "I cannot blame you, but he is a proud man, and a dangerous one."

"He tried to go around us, Jose. He needed to know that *we* are still in charge."

"Sí, Señor Presidente." Ansalmo smiled. "Are you ready for your meeting with the leaders of the assembly?"

"Sí, Jose. And I will inform them of our decision."

Then Vicente returned to his desk, plopped into his chair, and soon was smoking a second cigarette. His last two-cigarette day had involved a border incursion from Colombia mere months after his first inauguration.

Ansalmo stood opposite him, a hand leaned against the mahogany. "What about Lopez? Do you think he will operate behind our back?"

After a long drag on the cigarette, Vicente said, "Have Romero look into it."

Roberto Romero headed San Sebastiao's *Guardia Nacional,* making him their nation's top cop. Not only was Romero a lifelong member of law enforcement, he was Ansalmo's brother-in-law and, as such, had Vicente's trust.

The president said, "If Lopez is up to anything, Romero will find out about it . . . and, I have no doubt, stop him."

"*Sí, Señor Presidente,*" Ansalmo said. "I will assign him to the matter, immediately."

Vicente stubbed out his cigarette and rose. Pushing the button on his intercom, he said, "Have the car ready—I'll be right out."

A female voice came back, "*Sí, Señor Presidente.*"

The concern obvious in his voice, Ansalmo said, "I think you should be more careful, *Señor Presidente.*"

"All precautions are taken—you know that, Jose."

Ansalmo raised an eyebrow. "They may not be enough, sir. Too many people would seek to do you harm. We should double your security, and start using nonmilitary people, and perhaps even multiple vehicles."

"You worry too much, Jose." Vicente came around the desk and patted Ansalmo on the arm. "Get some rest, my friend—you look tired."

Ansalmo smiled. "*Señor Presidente,* if *I* am tired, you must be *exhausted.*"

With a grin, Vicente said, "Ah, you know what they say, Jose—no rest for the wicked. And even less rest for those who seek to stay *ahead* of the wicked. . . ."

They both chuckled; then the vice president walked Vicente out to his limousine.

Just before he climbed into the vehicle, Vicente said, "We are a good country with good people, Jose. A better day is ahead."

Ansalmo said, "I hope you are right, sir," and

the president got into the car, gave the order, and it drove off.

The ride to the national assembly meant three miles of weaving through the heavy traffic of the capital city, San Marco. At this time of day, traffic was at its most congested and even being the president of the country didn't help that much.

The motorcade was small, two motorcycle officers in front of an SUV of security men, the limo, another SUV of men, then two final motorcycles. The security team in the SUVs were members of Romero's *Guardia Nacional,* each handpicked by Romero for both ability and loyalty. There was an additional security man in the limo, up front with the specially trained driver. Presidente Vicente had the backseat to himself, his personal assistant having remained behind at the presidential palace.

Looking out the window, watching the cars around him as the good citizens of San Marco made their way home from another hard day of work, Vicente could not help but admire the perseverance of his people. Although it had yet to touch the capital, the threat of the rebels was real, but these people still went about their business, as if it were any other day.

Of course, the lack of rebel activity was also the reason why Vicente himself was traveling to the national assembly. Not only did it give the assembly leadership the notion that they had an advantage with him coming to their domain, it also allowed the citizens to see their president going about *his* business as usual.

The caravan turned right onto a street lined on

either side with office buildings. They were mostly newer structures, part of the modernization of San Marco and the beginning of Vicente's plan to upgrade the whole country. There was plenty of oil money to rebuild the entire country, update the schools, and refurbish the infrastructure, giving every citizen the opportunity for a better life.

The rebels thought the way to do that was through nationalizing oil and having the government provide for all the citizens. Vicente, Ansalmo, and those who believed in democracy were convinced thriving businesses would provide jobs for the populace, and spread the wealth through the free enterprise system.

Few knew, but Vicente had started working through back channels to get Ansalmo together with Benito Rojas, the rebel leader, to begin negotiating a cease-fire. The thought made Vicente smile. Such negotiations rendered the machinations of power-hungry generals and conscienceless arms dealers meaningless.

He was looking up at the buildings, thinking, despite it all, how bright the future looked for his nation, when he saw something flash from one of the rooftops.

The next thing he knew, one of the motorcycles ahead had slid down, its rider toppling off, the bike leaving a trail of sparks as it skittered down the street, metal screeching off pavement.

As Vicente tried to comprehend what was happening, the other motorcycle went down, and then he was flung back into his seat by a blinding flash followed by a *thud,* and he realized that the SUV ahead had blown up.

The security man in the front seat of the limo was screaming into his radio, "*Code red!* Code red! We're under *attack*!"

The driver jerked the limo right, to avoid the fireball of the SUV, and as they whizzed by, Vicente glimpsed a screaming silhouette, its arms flailing madly within the flame-filled vehicle.

Another massive *whoomp* followed, and a bright light came from behind Vicente—the rear SUV had blown up as well.

Still, Vicente could fight back the fear. The car was bulletproof, and his driver and security man were well trained. If that all failed, Vicente still felt calm. He had long ago made his peace with God.

As the driver wove through the wreckage and tried to get them clear, Vicente slipped down and was basically prone as he looked through the back-door window and saw a man on a rooftop aiming a gun at him, a weapon of a sort he had never seen before.

In that instant, Vicente realized that someone in his country already *had* pulse weapons . . . and that the trouble he had hoped to avoid was now squarely on his country's doorstep.

He saw the muzzle flash and wasn't the least bit surprised when the bulletproof window broke and an instant later something warm erupted from his chest.

Vincente thought of his wife and daughters and how much he loved them. Thoughts of his country would have followed, but he was already dead.

CHAPTER FOUR

Rip It Up

Quantico, Virginia

With bullets whistling overhead, Wallace Weems—Ripcord or Rip, to his friends and teammates—wondered why this was called the confidence course. He was up to his chin in the mud as he crawled beneath strands of barbed wire—live ammunition shrilling past less than a foot above his weave—and, right now, the *last* thing he felt was confidence.

Able Team was the best of the best and, consequently, their training ran longer, harder, and, well, *real*er than any other unit's. And this was starting to feel pretty damn real, about now. . . .

Feeling movement to his right, Rip glanced over to see his team leader, Duke Hauser, in the mud next to him.

"You gonna move?" Duke asked.

Another burst of gunfire whistled past their heads.

"Actually," Rip said, "it's pretty cozy right here."

"You're going to catch your death of cold," Duke said, in the singsong tone of an older brother.

"Death of lead poisoning, maybe," Ripcord said, shooting a glare at his best buddy. "From that dipstick with the machine gun."

Duke shook his head. "Sergeant Tanner is an expert marksman. You've got nothing to—"

Bullets tore up the mud in front of them, flecking their faces with thick brown teardrops.

As he wiped his face with his sleeve, Rip said, "What was that you were saying, Sunshine?"

Duke smirked. "Tanner boy's probably ready for a late lunch, and trying to get us to get our asses in gear. Can you blame him?"

"Yeah, I can blame him. This is me blaming him, right here." Rip shrugged. "Anyway, we could just have lunch where we are. You suppose Hooters delivers? Got my cellphone handy. I could make the call. Picnic time?"

Duke growled, "If you don't get your can moving, your next picnic will be in the stockade."

Shaking his head, Rip said, "You know, Duke, you can be one cold mother—"

Bullets ripped the mud in front of them again, coming right in where Isaac Hayes did in the *Shaft* theme, which coincidentally was Rip's ring tone.

"All right, all right!" Rip yelled. "I'm movin', I'm movin'!"

When the duo had completed the confidence course, Major Mark Heston—commander of their unit—was waiting. Tall, with a steel-bolt spine, gray sideburns, and gunmetal eyes that seemed to penetrate soul deep, Heston was known to be one "major" hard-ass—but fair. . . .

Eyes traveling from Ripcord to Duke, their team

lined up behind them, the major said, "Not your best effort."

"No, sir," Duke said.

"Perhaps you're all tuckered out from your last mission."

"That's it," Rip said quickly.

"Understandable. So, then, you'd like to try again?"

Ripcord could tell from the major's too-friendly tone, this was not a mere suggestion.

"Yes, sir," Duke said.

"I've got an even better idea, sir," Ripcord said. From the corner of an eye, he caught Duke's stricken look.

Major Heston turned more to Rip. "You do, soldier?"

"Yes, sir. Able is a top team and they weren't dogging it, sir—*I* was."

Rip got no argument on that score from either the major or Duke, though neither could hide their surprise at his admission.

"My idea is," Rip said, "you let me do the course again, solo, and I'll bet I get a better time this go-round."

The major almost managed to hide his amusement. "You have nothing to bet, Weems."

"Sir, we're scheduled for a twenty-four-hour leave after this. Suppose I bet my leave I can do better."

Heston's smile was cold. "I have a better bet, Weems. You do better, say *twenty-five percent* better, and the team gets its leave. You fail, you all are confined to base."

Ripcord could feel the eyes of his teammates drilling into him now. He really had been dogging it, but the team's total time was still well within acceptable range. Heston's wager would mean Ripcord would have to complete the course in near-record time.

"Yes, sir," Rip said. Because there was nothing else he could say.

Heston said, "Sergeant Tanner, your weapon please."

"Yes, sir," Tanner said, stepping forward and handing the machine gun to Heston, the sergeant not bothering to hide a wicked smile.

At the starting line, with Duke ready to send him off, Rip felt butterflies doing battle in his belly. He wasn't worried about the course, or even Major Heston firing live rounds at him. He just didn't want to let the team down.

"Any advice?" he asked Duke.

"How about," Duke said, "don't screw the pooch."

"Great. Just what I needed."

"Hey, *you* were the one dogging it. Now, the whole team's leave is on the line."

Tanner held the stopwatch, studying the thing; then his thumb came down and he yelled, *"Go!"*

Rip flew across the first fifty yards of open ground before the first obstacle, a cargo net stretched between a frame of four-by-fours that ran a good fifteen feet straight up.

He hit the rope ladder running, going hand over hand to the top, over, then down. He could feel sweat on his forehead, arms, and back as he hauled tail across fifteen yards of slightly sloped open ground, toward the next obstacle.

Three logs were stretched over a bog with about five feet between them, giving Rip the choice of which he wanted to take. He chose the one in the center and lowered his eyes, concentrating on taking three long strides and clearing the muck.

Next came one hundred and twenty yards of open ground, almost straight downhill this time, through trees and into a clearing where a single rope hung from a wooden A-frame, over a pond just wide enough that if he didn't swing all the way across, he was certain to take a muddy bath.

Sweat poured off him and his lungs burned as Rip tore down the hill, trying desperately not to take a limb to the face or trip over an exposed root.

As he neared the edge of the pond, Ripcord leapt, his arms extended to catch the rope. He caught the thing, nearly slipped down, then grabbed it tight as it swung him over the water, kicking wildly.

When he had cleared the pond, he let go and hit the ground, stumbling but maintaining his balance, then he was sprinting again. Ahead of him rose a fifteen-foot wooden wall with ropes as climbing aids.

Rip hit the wall with a foot, caught the rope, and pulled himself up quickly, hand over hand, walking up the wall. At the top, instead of climbing down the rope on the other side, Rip threw himself off, hit the ground, and did a somersault, springing to his feet and running up the next long hill.

That bought some seconds, he thought.

Over the crest waited the last obstacle, the barbed wire over the mud.

Major Heston would be there . . . with Tanner's machine gun.

Even as Rip crossed the hilltop and started down the other side, Heston opened fire, and bullets ripped the ground around Ripcord, these closer than Tanner ever dared get.

Diving into the mud, Rip scrambled through the nasty stuff, under the wire, careful to keep himself pressed into the mire as he tore through the final few yards.

Risking a look, he saw Major Heston aiming carefully, plowing the ground for planting within a foot of Rip, who rose from under the wire, sprinted the last fifteen yards, and crossed the line.

Tanner punched the button on the stopwatch.

"New course record," Tanner said to no one in particular, about as emotional as a guy checking out groceries.

Ripcord grinned as the team members stepped forward to slap him five.

"That didn't suck," Duke said.

"Yes," Major Heston said. "Well done, Weems."

"Thank you, sir," Rip said, standing a little straighter.

Heston called out: "You men have your leave!" Then, in an aside to Ripcord, he added, "And you better start figuring out what you're going to bet the *next* time you screw up."

"Won't happen again, sir," Rip said.

"This won't," Heston said. "But you'll think of something."

*   *   *

Two hours later, with the team scattered to hell and gone for the next twenty-four hours, Ripcord and Duke stepped out of an elevator onto the fourth floor of Walter Reed Army Medical Center in Washington, D.C.

Both men were in their Army dress uniforms—black jacket, navy-blue pants, white shirt, and black tie. Duke had a single shiny gold bar on each shoulder and wore an officer's cap. Ripcord wore a beret with the special forces logo, sergeant's stripes on his arms, hash marks near his left wrist. Each man had campaign ribbons, as well as various medals they'd earned.

The corridor was a clean hospital green with the distinct, clinging aroma of disinfectant. Not much traffic up here—a few nurses, the odd doctor, the occasional family member. The patients in this ward were in bad shape.

They found the room of David Westen, the team's medical officer, who'd been wounded on the Uzekurkistan mission. He shared a room with another gravely wounded soldier, who was beyond a separating curtain.

Rip looked down at their friend. Westen had never been the biggest guy to begin with. Now, with a ventilator breathing for him and an IV feeding him, the medic looked frailer yet. The edge of a bandage on Westen's chest peeked out from under his blanket. His eyes were shut, his beard untrimmed, his hair disheveled, but he appeared to be resting comfortably, despite the tubes snaking into his nose and mouth.

"Boy doesn't look that good," Rip said.

"Neither do you," Duke said, "but at least you're still up and walkin' around."

"You're just jealous. You *know* I look good. That cannot be denied."

And before Duke could deny it, an attractive Asian woman entered. Her black hair brushed the shoulders of a black turtleneck; she wore matching slacks and a white coat with the name "Dr. Chang" embroidered over the left breast, a stethoscope at her slender neck.

"May I help you, gentlemen?" she asked.

Ripcord bestowed on her what he hoped was his most winning grin. "I don't suppose you make house calls." He coughed dramatically. "Haven't been feelin' myself lately."

Her brown eyes bore into him, letting him know that he wouldn't be feeling her, either. "You're visiting this patient?"

Duke said, "Lieutenant Westen is the medical officer for our team. How is he doing, Doctor?"

Her expression grave, she said, "Dr. Westen *was* your team's medical officer. His combat mission days are over."

Duke nodded, then asked, "But will he be all right?"

Her eyebrows went up. "When he first got to Ramstein, they weren't sure he was going to pull through. Then, after twelve hours of surgery, he was placed in a medically induced coma—the state he remains in, while his wounds heal. A great deal of damage was done, and we decided this was the safest route for his rehabilitation . . . and the best opportunity for Lieutenant Westen to make a full recovery."

Rip put a hand on the doctor's nearest shoulder. "So, you're sayin' he's gonna *make* it."

"Yes," Dr. Chang said. "You, however, will end up in a room down the hall if those fingers do not disappear from my shoulder in the next three seconds."

"That isn't at all friendly, Doc. We're all in this together, right?"

"One," she said.

"What?"

"Two," she said.

Ripcord removed his hand. "Sorry."

Shaking his head, Duke said, "You'll have to excuse my friend here. He goes into politically incorrect mode every time he sees an attractive female."

"Dude," Rip said. "I'm standing right here. I'm in the *room*."

"*Neither* of you need to be in this room," Dr. Chang said. "Your friend doesn't know you're here, and you may be disturbing the patient in the next bed. If you don't mind?"

Dr. Chang was checking on Westen as they made their way out, Rip muttering about the doctor's bedside manner, and Duke saying, "Like *you'd* ever find out."

Outside, as they stood waiting for a taxi, Ripcord found himself thinking about things he had never really considered before.

He said to his friend, "What would you do if you didn't have the team?"

Duke studied Rip for a long moment. "Guess I never really thought about it. Why?"

"Well, someday we'll be too old for this game."

"Right. You don't play professional football forever."

"Yeah. And sometimes you go out early, on an injury. Take Westen—when he gets out of here, he won't have Able Team anymore."

"We're still his brothers," Duke said.

"Always will be," Ripcord said. "But we can't talk to him, about the missions we go on. I mean, they're mostly top secret. He may be our brother, but now he's dropped out of our world, and he can never get back in again."

"Point being?"

"Point being, question still stands—what would you do without the team?"

A taxi pulled up, they got in, and gave the driver the address of Tom and Harvey's, a Washington steak house with a national reputation.

When the vehicle got moving, Ripcord picked the thread back up: "You gonna answer my question or not?"

"Not sure I *know* the answer," Duke said. "Maybe you never noticed, but I'm not exactly the philosophical type."

"Yeah, I did notice. But hell, man, you must have *some* idea."

"Why? Do you?"

Rip thought about that, then grinned. "If I had to put the team behind me? I'd start over."

"Start over how? As what?"

"I don't know. Maybe . . . yeah, maybe I'd be a rapper."

"A rapper."

"Yeah, man. I listen to that stuff all the time. You know how much hip-hop I got on the ol' iPod?"

Duke grunted a laugh. "Yeah. Right. But unless you have a rifle in your hands, you've got the rhythm of a guy falling down the stairs. Plus the musical ability of a deaf-mute."

"That's *cold,* man," Rip said, but didn't deny it. He shrugged. "I didn't say there wouldn't be any challenges. I mean, I woulda done it already except . . . well . . . I ain't that good at rhymes."

"For a rapper I'd say that'd be a challenge, all right," Duke said. But his eyes said he was considering Rip's question about a future after Able Team. "Since the sky's the limit, then I guess I'd be quarterback."

"A quarterback. What team?"

"What else? St. Louis Rams."

Ripcord stared at him blankly. "I always knew you had a backup plan—somethin' to fall back on."

"Right," Duke said. "It was the Army or the NFL. The Army won."

"Lucky damn Army. Ever play ball in college?"

"No."

"High school? Middle school?"

"No. No. But you've seen me throw grenades. Do I have a deadly aim or not?"

"You're not bad."

"So if I can throw a grenade, then I can throw a football, right?"

Rip, not sure his friend could throw anything that wasn't about to imminently explode, changed the subject. "Is Ana going to meet us?"

A smile creased Duke's face. "Yeah. Rex, too."

Tall, lithe blonde Ana Lewis was Duke's girl-friend, and had been for over a year—getting really serious. Rex, a scientist and an Army major, was her older brother, whom Rip also knew well.

"Girl's too good for you," Ripcord said. "If I wasn't such a stand-up guy? I'd steal that sweet thing myself."

Duke smirked. "Sure. You could rap to her under her window and win her right over."

"Hey, I got moves."

A grin cracked Duke's face. "Like the ones you laid on Dr. Chang? Smooth, bro. *Smooth*. . . ."

"Hey, she was into me!"

Ana and Rex were waiting on the sidewalk in front of Tom and Harvey's. Spring hadn't quite come to D.C. yet, but the weather was warm with just a faint chill noticeable when the breeze kicked in; still, no one had bothered with an overcoat this evening.

Ana wore a dark waistcoat over a plain black silk blouse, and a long black skirt with a slit ac-centing her long, shapely legs; her straight blonde hair touched her shoulders, high cheekbones high-lighting a heart-shaped face made even prettier by an effervescent smile and startling blue eyes.

Rip greeted Ana with a quick hug and she re-sponded with a soft kiss on his cheek.

"Rip," she said, beaming, "it's so good to see you! Keeping out of trouble?"

"I've been with your guy here," he said, flicking a thumb toward Duke. "I been in nothing *but* trouble."

She smirked. "Do you two ever say anything nice about each other?"

"Well, the dude has a beautiful girlfriend. Give him that."

She gave Rip another kiss, and he thought, *Man, I do have moves. . . .*

From just behind and to one side of her, Rex Lewis took a step. "Ten-*hut!*"

Rex wore an Army dress uniform as well, major's gold oak leaves within white-bordered epaulets on his shoulders. The resemblance between Ana and her brother showed up mostly in the similar shape of their faces; what they had most in common was a keen intelligence.

Rip snapped to attention, saluted, then before Rex could return the salute, Rip laughed out loud and threw his arms around Rex. "How ya doin', Major?"

Chuckling as he hugged back, Rex said, "That's no way to treat a superior officer."

"You could always give me a field promotion."

"Why would I do that?"

"So I can treat you with the disrespect you deserve!"

Rex laughed at that, and the two had their arms around each other's shoulders. So did Duke and Ana, but in a different way—the pair was lost in a deep embrace and deeper kiss.

Rip raised a lecturing finger. "Rex, my man, this is where a good brother steps in and cleans the clock of the guy takin' liberties with his sister."

"The Navy takes liberties, Rip," Rex said. "The *Army* takes leave. And we should leave them to it."

"Fair enough," Rip said, making sure Duke and Ana heard him. "But this is a city street, and there *are* laws. . . ."

Finally Duke stopped hugging Ana and started hugging Rex, saying, "I thought you were off someplace, saving the world through science."

Ripcord grinned and jerked a thumb at his chest, saying to Duke, "Hey, I thought saving the world was *our* job."

"You in your way," Rex said. "Me in mine."

Rip said, "Well, our way is killing all the bad guys. You may have something more humane in mind."

They entered the bustling steak house and were seen by the maître d' past the enclosed bar through the boisterous dining room to their reserved table. No one took notice of three men in military dress uniforms, a common sight in D.C., and anyway, the president himself was among the occasional clientele. It was the beautiful woman gliding across the room who caught so much interest—everything seemed to slow down, men trying not to gawk and failing, women trying not to stare with equal lack of success, and the murmur of conversation and clink of china and glassware subsiding ever so slightly.

The beige walls of the brightly lit dining room were trimmed in dark oak with crown molding, one wall dominated by a painting of six jazz musicians featuring Louis Armstrong on trumpet, Earl "Fatha" Hines playing a serpentine keyboard, Woody Herman on clarinet, and Jack Teagarden on trombone. There were two other jazz musicians depicted, but Rip didn't recognize them.

Still, for a guy of his generation, Rip had a particularly strong knowledge of jazz, and he asked the maître d', "The bass and guitar player—who are those cats?"

Over his shoulder, he said, "Our namesakes— Tom is on the bass, Harvey on the guitar."

The walls were lined with green banquettes, the tables adorned with white tablecloths and fresh-cut flowers. Throughout the middle of the room, diners sat on wooden chairs around square tables, and it was to one of these that the maître d' led them.

Before long a perky, buxom blonde waitress in a tuxedo shirt, bow tie, and black slacks took their orders. She was attractive enough that Duke gave Rip a warning look, and Rip behaved himself. The only incident involved ordering wine—Rex had taken over, saying, "Allow me."

Rex apparently considered himself a wine connoisseur, but Rip had never been to a fancy restaurant with the guy, and had no idea if Rex actually knew squat.

"We'd like a bottle of Pahlmeyer merlot," Rex said. "The '03, I believe."

The waitress complimented him on his choice and went away.

Rip gave the medical major half a grin and said,

"Am I supposed to believe you weren't just *fakin'* that?"

"You'll taste it and apologize. Wait and see. That is, assuming you know anything about any wine that doesn't come with a screw-on cap."

Duke said, "Or in a box, maybe."

Ana and Duke shared little smiles, and Rip took it like a man.

"The Pahlmeyer," Rex said, "is a good wine, a *very* good wine—for a California one, anyway."

"Man," Rip said, "I woulda never took you for such a snob."

His smile still firmly in place, Rex said, "Is it snobbery to want the best? To think that we work hard and deserve something for our service to our country? I don't think so."

Rip let it go—it was a social evening, and he didn't want to ruin it for Duke and Ana, and anyway, Rex was a nice guy, even if he had revealed a patronizing streak.

Anyway, Ripcord Weems *did* want the best, and not just in what he ate and drank. He wanted to *be* the best, which was why he had joined up in the first place—though being the best was not an easy job when you were always teamed up with a guy like Duke Hauser, who seemed to have excellence in his damn DNA.

The sommelier brought the wine; Rex tasted it and pronounced it fit for them to drink. Their glasses were filled and they raised them.

Duke made the toast. "To our brothers."

They all followed suit. "To our brothers."

Ana was looking at Rex.

And the damn wine was good indeed. Rip even admitted as much to Rex. The conversation, as they waited for their food to arrive, was light and breezy, although at one point, Ana did ask Duke about Doc Westen.

"He's going to be all right," Duke said. "But his days with the team are over."

Ana frowned in concern. "That's awful for him. And probably not so easy for you."

Shrugging, Duke said, "We all know that casualties go with the job."

Placing a hand on his, Ana said, "I know. But what I meant was—"

"We *will* miss him," Duke said, anticipating her. "But we're paid to keep doing what we're supposed to do. And we'll do that. It's what we've always done."

Ana was studying him with compassionate but also curious eyes. "Then you're . . . all right?"

"I'm fine," Duke said.

"Yeah, me, too, I'm great," Rip said. "Thanks for asking."

They all laughed at that.

They were halfway through their meals when Rex asked, "Has your team been assigned a new medic yet?"

Duke shook his head.

Rex straightened; his smile was a thin, confident line. "Then I've still got time to put in for a transfer."

Ana turned to him, her eyes wide, even alarmed. "You're not a *doctor,* Rex, you're a scientist! You're not trained for combat—"

"Actually, I am," Rex said, cutting her off. "I have more than enough medical training to qualify as a medic."

Ana seemed astounded and not in a good way. "But why would you *want* to?"

His expression was somber. "I want to be seen as more than just a glorified lab rat. I want to help, really do my share, Sis—I want to be part of the *solution*."

Ana looked perplexed. "To what problem?"

"To *all* the problems in this godforsaken world."

Duke said, "Hey, buddy—can't you do that in the lab? Won't you do more good there?"

Rex gave a little shrug. "Eventually. But while I'm young, I should experience the real world, not just the sterile one that I'm fated to spend most of my life in."

Rip said, "Hey, you got a good gig goin'. Don't screw it up, son."

Rex shook his head, insistent. "No, Rip. Right now I feel like I could do more good out in the field. Don't ask me for a logical explanation—it's just a *feeling* I have."

They were all staring at Rex now, Rip wondering what the hell was in that wine anyway.

"A scientist tellin' us to throw logic out the window," Ripcord said. "Merlot—what *is* that? French for 'drunk on your butt after one sip'?"

Rex smiled a little, but his tone remained somber: "Laugh at me if you like, Rip. But this is how I feel. I have a good idea of just how much you and Duke have accomplished, and I want a piece of that. I want to make the kind of difference you guys make."

Rip made a face. "You want to trade in your doctor's bag for a machine gun?"

Shaking his head, Rex said, "I don't want to hurt anybody. I just want to be medical support, like Westen."

Ana, softly, said, "Like Westen in *intensive care*, you mean?"

Rex ignored that.

Duke sat forward, pushing his mostly eaten plate of food aside. "Rex, hurting people is what we do for a living. Worse than that—killing people."

Eyes narrowing, Rex said, "You told me once that you guys didn't just take lives, you also saved them. Remember?"

Ana turned to Duke, giving him a dark look that was somehow accusing.

With a shrug, Duke said, "We try to save lives. That's the goal, yes."

"Well, I want to be part of that," Rex said. "The lab has its place, and someday—"

They were interrupted by the chirp of Duke's cellphone.

He excused himself, stepping away from the table, and then Rip's cell rang as well, the first few bars of "The Theme from Shaft." Rip followed Duke into a hallway, Duke answering first and already talking to somebody when Rip hit the button on his phone.

"*Weems?*"

"Who's this?"

"*Major Heston. It's a code red, Weems. Leave ends right now.*"

"Yes, sir! On my way, sir!"

"*You're with Hauser?*"

"Yes, sir."

"*How long to get back to base?*"

"We'll have to get a cab, sir. Could be two hours."

"*Get moving, then. If you're still sitting down, you're wasting time!*"

"I'm standing, sir. And leaving right now. . . ."

When they got back to Quantico, the rest of the team was already assembled in the briefing room, short of Stearns and Bergman, who entered less than ten minutes after Rip and Duke.

The room was set up with two rows of tables, each with two chairs, reminding Rip of a high-school science class. The nine men of Able Team sat in pairs, Duke and Rip at the one front-row table while Sterns and Bergman wound up with the other front seats, the early arrivals having had the good sense to sit toward the rear.

Major Heston came in through a side door, with a Hispanic corporal in fatigues close behind him.

As the ranking man in the room, Duke rose and said, "Ten-*hut*!"

They rose as one and saluted.

Heston gave them a hasty salute as he moved to the front of the room and said, "As you were."

The team sat.

A lectern held a laptop computer hooked up to a projector aimed at the screen beside the major. He picked up a remote and looked out over them.

"First things first," Heston said. "This is your new medic—Arturo Benitez."

The medic smiled and nodded, but did not otherwise move. He wore his black hair high and tight, and had wide-set brown eyes with a Broadway brightness that matched his smile.

"Take a seat, Benitez," Heston said.

The new recruit took a seat halfway back, sharing a table with Ray Peters, a stocky, sure-shot sniper from Iowa.

Heston punched a button on the remote and a map of northern South America popped onto the screen.

Using a laser pointer, the major said, "This is San Sebastiao. It's a small democracy that's in big trouble. Their president, Martin Vicente, has been assassinated. Going into San Sebastiao was your next mission scheduled, and at the end of your leave, it would have kicked in. But we've had to cancel your leave and move this up. Why?"

No one reacted in any way, but something in the air seemed charged now.

Heston continued: "The vice president, Jose Ansalmo, has disappeared, and the leader of the military, General Pedro Lopez, has taken control of the country . . . and he's enforcing martial law. He is, in fact, blaming *Ansalmo* for plotting the assassination of President Vicente. This is Vice President Ansalmo. . . ."

The map was replaced on the screen by the image of a handsome Hispanic gentleman with a goatee.

Duke said, "Excuse me, sir, but you don't sound

convinced that the vice president is behind the assassination."

"I'm not at all convinced Ansalmo's responsible. Our intel is that General Lopez himself pulled those strings."

Now on the screen was a curly-haired military man.

"Or," the captain continued, "at the very least, Lopez was aware of the plot, particularly if it was hatched by an international arms merchant named Emile Chernitz . . ."

The screen now belonged to a fortyish man with a salt-and-pepper beard.

". . . who has been reported to have been in Lopez's company at the presidential palace, in the aftermath of the assassination, and the general's taking control of the government."

"Banana republic stuff," Duke said.

"I wish that were all it was," Heston said. "The weapons used to assassinate President Vicente were next-gen pulse rifles."

Rip frowned. "Excuse me, sir. But what are those?"

" 'Those' are—in the short version—weapons utilizing a magnetic pulse to speed up a nonmagnetic projectile, which not only makes it fly faster but straighter, too. Not to mention the explosive tips."

Now on the screen was a bombed-out street like the worst war-torn landscape out of the Middle East; but instead it was the scene on the South American street where Vicente's assassination had gone down.

Rip began, "What the hell kind of—"

"Just leave it at 'hell,' Sergeant Weems," Heston said. "It's some kind of hell."

Duke asked, "What's our interest in this, sir?"

The major sighed. "With the trouble in the Middle East—and keeping in mind the other oil-producing South American countries who seem to hate Uncle Sam—San Sebastiao has been a friendly source for reasonably priced oil. They've had trouble with rebels, but that was minor compared to this, an apparent military coup. If the rebels *or* Lopez take and maintain control, our country could be hit by the worst oil crisis since Jimmy Carter was in the White House."

Duke asked, "What can our team do?"

Heston paused momentarily. His commanding voice became hushed: "This is not a normal insertion action. What we have in mind for this is something more . . . covert. This will be strictly a volunteer operation."

Of course, all of Able Team volunteered, although Duke and Rip were, as always, first in line.

CHAPTER FIVE
Duke It Out

The Pit

Ninety-nine percent of the world was unaware that G.I. JOE even existed. The other one percent was about evenly divided between the JOEs themselves (and their allies), and those who would destroy G.I. JOE and the positive influence it attempted to exert.

General Hawk, on the other hand, was aware of about ninety-nine percent of the plots against G.I. JOE and its allies. What worried him was that other one percent.

This business in San Sebastiao, of course, was something he knew about—up to a point. He had hoped to have his team on the ground before anything happened to President Vicente, but someone else's plan had progressed faster than Hawk's JOEs could react.

On a computer screen at his desk in his stateroom office, Hawk studied scores of stills taken at the assassination site, from professional photographers to cellphones and everything in between. Most were shot immediately after the tragedy, others in the aftermath when fire and smoke no longer clouded the landscape.

The general knew that if Chernitz's weapons had been trucked out of Uzekurkistan, they must have soon been loaded onto a ship bound for South America. He'd even known what the likely ship had been, and satellites were still tracking that very vessel . . . and yet pulse weapons had been used to assassinate President Vicente.

That meant either Chernitz had fooled them, or there were more pulse weapons than G.I. JOE or anyone else knew about. The capabilities of such weapons chilled the battle-hardened general, and more chilling yet were the whispers that the next generation of pulse weapons promised to leave conventional firepower behind, replacing bullets with sheer subatomic blasts that could rip men and machines apart like a child tearing paper.

There had been at least three pulse rifles at the assassination scene, but those may simply have been prototypes smuggled out earlier, separate from the Uzekurki shipment. That, anyway, was Hawk's hope.

But the possibility that a larger quantity of these formidable weapons might be coming into play was despair-inducing. Unit Alpha needed to nip this damn thing in the bud, else the balance of power in South America might be catastrophically tipped.

Worse yet, JOE intel had been unable to verify that the assassins weren't rebels. Meaning they could not be sure which side of the San Sebastioan conflict had control of at least three pulse weapons.

With more on the way, *both* sides could wind up with the extreme armaments, and the death and destruction would expand beyond military action into massive civilian casualties.

Hawk knew the U.S. military was sending Able Team in to deal with the political situation. He even knew the plan, and thought it might just work—the team was, after all, aptly named, with both Hauser and Weems JOE-worthy material.

His real problem was the weapons themselves—San Sebastiao staying a friendly democratic regime in the region was of course a good thing, but *not* more important than securing the armaments. That was the objective of Unit Alpha, the G.I. JOE team. In a perfect world, they could have both; the democracy intact and the weapons confiscated or destroyed. Hawk, however, knew the world was many things, but perfect was not one of them.

Cover Girl leaned in and knocked on the open door. He bid her enter. As usual, her uniform was immaculate, her hair swept up in a severe bun, her tablet computer resting on her left forearm.

"Yes?" Hawk said, his eyes still on the monitor.

"Unit Alpha is on the ground, sir."

"Good. Any problems?"

"Breaker reports the situation is a-okay, thus far."

"Do we know where they are?"

"I can show you, sir."

He motioned her behind his desk as he kept clicking through assassination scene images; finally a map of San Sebastiao took over the screen.

Cover Girl leaned in and pointed, saying, "Right there, sir."

San Sebastiao

After the dry heat of the Sahara, the relative autumnal cool of the San Sebastiaoan jungle seemed a pleasant change of pace for unit leader Gung Ho.

In fact, the humidity of the tropics—even with the Southern Hemisphere's summer fading—reminded Ettienne R. LaFitte of his boyhood days growing up in Fer de Lance, Louisiana. In its own way, the sweat-soaking of his fatigues felt comforting. He had black camouflage makeup on, just as Scarlett and Breaker did, to reduce the moonlight shine on their white faces.

The team was cold camping—no fires, fifteen klicks northwest of San Marco. Somewhere out there, Snake Eyes was patrolling the perimeter, a silent sentinel. Heavy Duty sat under a tree, his MPHW Gatling-style gun within easy reach, his eyes closed. Breaker, who had just radioed HQ, stretched out on the ground, his pack under his head as he prepared to catch some sleep as well. Not far from Gung Ho, Scarlett sat swigging water from her canteen.

His voice low, Gung Ho said, "I'd be happier if we'd met our contact by now."

Wiping her mouth with the sleeve of her fatigues, Scarlett said, "It'll happen when it happens."

"Since when are you philosophical?" Gung Ho knew the young woman prided herself on her cool logic and no-nonsense scientific bent.

Scarlett shrugged. "I guess it comes with hanging out with Snake Eyes. Kind of crept in by osmosis."

"Really? Snake doesn't *talk*."

The lovely redhead gave him half a smile. "You have to *talk* to be a philosopher?"

Gung Ho had no answer for that. "You should get some sleep. Who knows when we'll get another chance."

"Sounds like good advice. What about you?"

He plopped down not far from her. "I'm going to catch some z's, too. Snake Eyes will stay awake enough for all of us."

"Nice to have a philosopher," Scarlett said with a tilt of her head, "who knows his way around a blade. . . ."

Gung Ho went out as soon as his eyes closed— he had that ability, just to switch off his inner lights, a real gift for a fighting man.

But he didn't know how long he'd been asleep when he sensed someone moving around. He slit his eyes open; not dawn yet. Whoever it was was damn close to him. Priming himself, Gung Ho tried to keep his body relaxed so the intruder wouldn't know the Louisiana brawler was about to pounce. . . .

A hand touched his shoulder and Gung Ho rolled and grabbed; but his attacker was too quick, stepping back to evade him.

Now Gung Ho could make out the silhouette of Snake Eyes, the ninja commando staring off toward the edge of their camp.

Whispering, Gung Ho said, "Friend or foe?"

Snake Eyes, naturally, said nothing.

But it was answer enough, just seeing that Snake

Eyes was making no move to wake the rest of the team. Whoever was headed toward them was not an enemy.

Their contact—it had to be.

"Incoming friendlies," Gung Ho said, keeping his voice low.

Still, that's all it took to wake the rest, who at once went from sound sleep to ready for action. Checking his watch, Gung Ho calculated he'd gotten four hours of sleep. Felt like less, but that didn't matter now.

Before their guests arrived, Heavy Duty took his big weapon and disappeared into the jungle at the edge of the camp. Snake Eyes, likewise, melted into the undergrowth, while Scarlett and Breaker remained at the campsite with their unit leader.

A moment later, two young people walked slowly into their midst. Even in the darkness, Gung Ho could tell one was a young man, the other a woman, both in their early twenties, painfully thin, and with the dark complexions and black hair of Quichans, a tribe native to San Sebastiao. Both wore camouflage slacks, sneakers, and olive drab T-shirts, and carried strap-slung AK–47s over their shoulders.

And they looked terrified.

"*Hola,*" the young man said, a tiny quaver in his voice.

Despite the tropical predawn darkness, Gung Ho said, "Chilly day."

"*Sí,*" the young man said. "But at lease de sun, it ees shining."

Despite the young man's broken English, Gung

Ho easily caught the kid's response to the code phrase.

Offering his hand, he said, "They call me Gung Ho."

"Joaquin," the kid said, and they shook hands. The kid had a feeble smile going, his fear easing to mere nervousness. "Thees ees my seester, Antonia."

The girl gave them a tiny smile, but said nothing.

Joaquin said, "She ees shy. Her English, she no so good like mine."

"Right," Gung Ho said.

"You are heere to save our country, yes?"

"We're going to take a swing at it," Gung Ho said.

The boy frowned at him.

Gung Ho tried again: "We're here to save your country—yes."

Joaquin beamed. "*Bueno*. Than we must go—quickly."

Loud enough for the whole team to hear, Gung Ho said, "Yo, JOEs! Saddle up."

Duke's team would be coming into San Sebastiao in two waves.

The first half, including Duke and Ripcord, had landed this afternoon, the sunshine bright, the temperature in the low eighties, even though fall had fallen down here. Each man traveled alone, flying commercially, and staying in a different hotel, with the exception of Duke and Rip, who had reservations for adjoining rooms in the El Presidente, the finest accommodations in San Marco, despite the topical irony of its name.

The airport seemed surprisingly modern, at least till Duke remembered just how much oil money was pouring into the little country. The taxi, on the other hand, was a twenty-five-year-old Chevy with threadbare seats and lousy suspension, no doubt getting the kind of mileage that could cause a one-car gas shortage.

The mission Major Heston had outlined to them back at Quantico hinged upon Able Team going in not as a military unit, but more as covert operatives.

"*Mission: Impossible* style," Rip had said, and ever since had been punctuating conversations with his version of the old *dum dum DUM DUM dum dum DUM DUM* theme song.

Sometimes Duke didn't know whether having Rip for a friend made him want to laugh or cry. He'd been teamed on basic training with Rip, and really didn't like the guy, found him cocky and grating; then on their first mission together, Rip had taken a bullet for Duke, and they had been friends ever since.

Anyway, their cover was that they were mercenaries seeking employment in the San Sebastiaoan civil war. Intel indicated that General Lopez was supplementing his military forces with an army of mercenaries on the side.

Duke and his team, showing up individually, would seek employment in the general's little side project, and that would give them a gateway to search for Vice President Ansalmo, the rightful leader of the country . . . assuming, of course, the V.P. was still alive.

Consequently, when they stepped from the rickety taxi, neither man was in uniform—Ripcord wore khaki cargo shorts, a Knicks T-shirt, and sneakers with no socks, while the more conservative Duke wore khaki cargo pants and a black Polo, sleeves barely containing his muscular arms. His black boots were, as usual, shined to a mirror polish.

Taking in the stately facade of the ten-story stone hotel, Ripcord said, "Man, you know, every mission ought to be like this. Call this mission *possible,* baby."

"Don't be fooled," Duke said quietly. "This is a military operation."

"Yeah, it is, except 'stead of sleeping on the ground in the jungle? We be livin' large."

" 'Living large' worries me," Duke said. "Makes us easier to see. Give me the jungle."

"Relax, Tarzan—you'll get to kick just as much behind as normal. Maybe you just won't have to do it wearin' camouflage and carrying fifty pounds of gear."

"I like my fifty pounds of gear," Duke said. "Especially my M16."

"I can see that. A dude needs a good luck charm. . . ."

They wheeled suitcases behind them as they approached the entrance, where a man in a uniform worthy of General Lopez greeted them with an *"Hola,"* and opened the bronze-framed door for them.

The El Presidente's lobby belonged more in a palace than a hotel—marble floors and columns, lavish rugs, and Louis XIV furniture. Again Duke was reminded of the oil money that flowed through the San Sebastiao economy.

"This place does not suck," Ripcord said. "This place, I could get used to."

Around them, businessmen, tourists, and diplomats made their way through the lobby, and Rip and Duke stuck out some. But they weren't alone in their casual attire or their hard-bitten features, either: other tough-looking male "tourists" lounging in chairs and on sofas were sizing them up.

The competition, Duke thought.

Mercs who, like them, were seeking employment in Lopez's army . . . or who already had jobs with the general, and were now working as his secret police, keeping tabs on the guests at the hotel.

"Over there," Duke said softly, indicating a guy with a shiny, shaved head, seated on a sofa perhaps fifteen feet away.

The man's apparel was similar to Duke's, but for a flimsy sports coat stretched to its limit by an overly developed upper torso. He was reading a magazine, but his eyes kept leaving the text to casually check out the new American arrivals.

"Glock in a shoulder holster under his left arm," Rip said, his lips barely moving. "You're slowin' down, Duke—I spotted the boy ten steps ago."

"What about the one on our right?"

This one was Latino, almost as large as the first one. He loitered near a coffee bar opposite the check-in counter. The hotel was air-conditioned and, like his buddy across the way, this dude wore a sportscoat.

"Yeah, I made him too," Rip said, "and the gun's under his left arm, but at this distance I can't tell what kind."

They checked in. Their reservations had been made by the Army, but through so many false fronts, there was no way for Lopez or anyone else to trace them.

Keycard in hand, Duke started toward the elevator.

"Place is crawling with secret police," Duke said with a humorless smirk.

"You got that right."

They stepped off the elevator at the ninth floor and found their rooms. Duke felt fortunate that he wasn't superstitious—his room was 913 and Rip had 911—although, for a moment, for some reason, he wondered just how secure their covers were.

Duke used the keycard and went in. The walls were eggshell white, the furniture continuing the lobby's Louis XIV theme but with the modern touch of a wall-mounted flat-screen TV. The bed was smaller than San Sebastiao, just barely, and its green floral bedspread recalled the jungle he'd said he would prefer to all this luxury.

Maybe Rip was right, and he *was* nuts.

The door between Duke's room and Rip's opened and his neighbor burst in, a bottle of beer from the minibar already in his hand. "Is this the best duty ever, or what?"

Shaking his head, Duke said, "Your Uncle Sammy isn't so rich that he's gonna spring for two-hundred-*peseta cervezas* from the minibar."

"Uncle who?" Rip asked.

Duke glanced around the room and Rip caught on.

They spent the next hour sweeping the two rooms for bugs, making idle small talk as they went. The only thing either came up with in these immaculate rooms was a dust bunny under Rip's bed.

Duke said, "Better get some rest."

Rip grinned. "Now you're talking. I can't wait to hit that fancy rack."

Duke raised a lecturing forefinger. "Don't forget—we're supposed to be at the rendezvous at twenty-two hundred tonight."

"The only question I've got," Rip said, "is do we want to have dinner downstairs first? Charging it to *El Room-o*."

Duke grimaced. "You better get focused, buddy boy."

Rip's manner was easygoing as he put a hand on his buddy's shoulder. "Hey, my man—just 'cause we're surrounded by a bunch of merc jerks, who would gladly rip us to shreds just to see what color we are inside, that doesn't mean a man should go without dinner. Now, do you want to go downstairs for some surf and turf about eight, or what?"

Duke let loose a big laugh—his first since he and Rip had left Ana and Rex unceremoniously at the steak house in D.C.

"All right, all right," Duke said. "You win."

"I *always* win."

"More often than not, you do."

With Rip gone, and left to some peace and quiet, Duke stowed his clothes in the dresser and his shaving kit in the bathroom. No point in turning on the television since his Spanish was too weak to understand much of it. Instead, he plopped down on the bed.

When he heard the knock at his door, his eyes opened to find the room bathed in darkness, moonlight filtering through the sheer curtains. He sat up and rubbed the back of his neck. Sleep had come easily and deeply. He felt groggy but refreshed.

From beyond the connecting door, Rip's voice said: "It's me," over another round of knocking.

"Yeah, yeah," Duke said. He reached over and switched on the bedside lamp.

Rip had changed into black cargo pants and a black Oakland Raiders T-shirt.

Duke asked, "Couldn't find your 'Kill 'em all, let God sort 'em out' T-shirt?"

"Savin' that for tomorrow night."

"Let's hope Lopez is looking for idiot mercenaries."

Dinner was good, steak for Duke, surf and turf for Rip. They let themselves be seen throwing around a little money; mercenaries liked the good life, when they weren't killing for money.

After, they walked the streets of the capital, winding up outside a bar called El Gato Negro. Whether or not this Black Cat was an omen of bad luck remained to be seen. . . .

They entered the gloomy bar and Duke could only wonder if they were in the wrong place. To call it a dive would be an insult to the many dives Duke had known around the world. The floor wasn't dirt, nor was it any recognizable man-made covering either. Might have been tile or concrete at some point in distant days past, but the crusty surface likely hadn't been swept since a Roosevelt had occupied the White House—possibly Teddy, not Franklin.

The walls were a mottled gray, bare of pictures, posters, or any kind of artwork save the stains of drinks that had been heaved over the years, and a few neon signs behind the bar. The tables were rickety, the chairs worse, the bar itself like something out of an old Western, except the bullet holes looked real. A jukebox with a cracked glass facade played Tex-Mex rock 'n' roll, fighting to be heard over raucous conversations at various tables.

A pot-bellied bald Latino in his fifties stood behind the bar wiping out glasses with a towel that may also have done double-duty cleaning the toilet, assuming the latter had ever been cleaned. Opposite him, a couple of women either in their thirties or in the midst of very hard twenties were either hookers or waitresses—maybe both. Whatever the case, with their scoop-necked peasant blouses and skintight black slit skirts, the only mystery left was where they kept the cigarettes they constantly lighted up, stubbed out, and lighted up.

A couple of brave but seasoned tourists occupied seats at the bar down from the women. Several more groups, mostly lowlife-looking men, were scattered at tables around a barroom about the size of a two-car garage. Whatever oil money was pouring into San Sebastiao, it had slid right by El Gato Negro.

Although Heston's intel had clearly pointed to this joint as the prime recruiting spot for Lopez's mercenary force, Duke was having his doubts. . . .

He and Rip took a table, and when one of the waitresses wandered over and asked, *"Que?"* Rip said, *"Dos cervezas, señorita."*

She gave Rip a lecherous smile that reminded Duke of the kind his pal usually offered good-looking women. Turnabout was fair play, they said.

Just as their beers arrived, Duke looked up to see Benitez stroll in. The skinny medic wore jeans and a white button-down shirt with the long sleeves folded up to his elbows. He was serving both as their translator and their medic on this mission, but Duke wished the unit's newbie had remained in his hotel room for this part of it.

Not that Benitez might not be needed here in one, or both, of his capacities. . . .

The beer was bottled, something called Pizzaro. As Rip paid for the beers, he said to Duke, "Notice I'm not makin' a bad men's room joke or anything."

"Your restraint is appreciated."

Benitez took a lonely stool down at the end of the bar.

Rip and Duke nursed their Pizzaros, chatting about nothing, Duke wondering how many nights it would take of this before they could make a meaningful contact. And how many nasty encounters with bad-ass locals would happen along the way. . . .

As he considered this, Stearns and Bergman entered, taking a table off to Duke's left. Over the next hour or so, they all sat around drinking, but none having more than two beers. Slowly, the place filled, things not really getting revved up until at least midnight at a joint like this.

Duke kept a head count, and a measure of who he considered potential allies and enemies, and those he was unsure of. By the time the witching hour struck, he'd added up twenty-three non-allies, not including the two floozies working as waitresses.

Five against twenty-three didn't seem like particularly good odds, but didn't really worry Duke. His team, even just four of them and a medic, were combat pros. One or two of these guys might be mercs, but most of the rest looked like ordinary rabble. Ordinary rabble didn't scare Duke. He'd had his rabies shots.

"Man," Rip said. "This could take awhile."

Duke shrugged.

The scantily clad waitress came back. *"Un otro?"* she asked.

"Sí," Rip said, holding up two fingers. *"Dos mas."*

The waitress wandered off and a minute later returned with two more Pizzaros. She set them on the table, her hand grazing Rip's and staying there a second longer than necessary.

Duke conceded that the woman might have been a looker if she combed that black rat's nest and either bought some new teeth or at least kept her mouth shut. Rip seemed to have no problem with her looks—he'd always graded on a curve.

As Rip appreciatively watched her hip-sway off,

the biggest man in the room rose and headed their way—a blockheaded giant wearing a sleeveless green T-shirt and jeans, at least a head taller than Duke, who wasn't exactly a shrinking violet. Duke wondered if they were getting lucky and were about to get a quick contact, or if the luck of the black cat meant this character was just a local nuisance.

The guy went right past Duke and rested a sausage-fingered hand on Rip's arm.

Looking up into the guy's mud-brown eyes, Rip asked, "*Que pasa,* my brother?"

The guy's black hair hung down like sick seaweed. He grinned at Rip. "You hitting on my *esposa, amigo?*"

Rip sat back a little, surprised. *"Esposa?"* he asked, glancing toward Duke.

"Wife," Duke supplied.

"I know what it means," Rip said, irritably. But he said to the guy in English, "You're a lucky man. And she has a *job,* too."

The guy looked perplexed as Rip took a casual swig of beer, indicating the conversation was over.

Then the waitress's better half said, "You would look good with your head on a stick."

"It's true. I *always* look good," Rip said, and spun the bottle in his hand and broke it across the giant's nose.

The big man straightened, blood pouring from twin spigots. To Rip and Duke's chagrin, however, the bloody-faced giant merely smiled at them—unlike his wife, he had all his teeth, and they were very yellow, and not just the gold ones.

"Aw hell," Ripcord said.

"I was just thinking that," Duke said.

And they both jumped to their feet as everyone in the bar seemed to move at once.

The big man with the bloody nose took a wild swing at Rip, who countered by picking up a second beer bottle and smashing it down on the brute's head. Another cut opened, blood erupting down his forehead like red wet bangs, but the guy kept coming.

Worse yet, *El Hubbo* kept grinning.

Meanwhile, two other guys were charging Duke.

The first, a mean-looking little man with a scar on one cheek and a switchblade in one hand, was met by Duke's left to the sternum, which slowed him, then a right to the chin, which dropped him.

The second guy swung a fist down with his knife, the blade arcing, bar neon glinting off steel. Duke blocked the blow with his forearm against his assailant's, sending the knife clattering somewhere, then followed with a knife-edge hand to the man's throat, putting his assailant down, hands gripping his gurgling throat, as if trying to strangle himself.

Over near the bar, Benitez was surrounded by four guys; Duke moved in to help him.

Elsewhere, the big man in front of Ripcord still grinned, almost manically, his face a bloody mask. A switchblade appeared in one fat fist and snicked open, like a serpent's tooth extending for the kill.

As the knife sliced toward him, Ripcord kicked, his boot meeting the man's arm, sending the blade flying as Rip pivoted and delivered a reverse kick to the man's groin.

The sound that came out of the big *hombre* was somewhere between a squeak and a scream, as all the air *whooshed* out of him, and he sagged to his knees. Husband of the Year wasn't grinning now—he just looked up dumbly, numbly, in time to see Rip driving a chair down. The chair exploded over the guy's skull, and he was unconscious before he hit the floor.

Benitez's eyes were wide with fear as he tried to keep moving to keep the four guys off him. Duke waded in, kicking one in the back of the knee, then cracking the bastard across the face with a beer bottle as he fell.

The nearest assailant turned toward Duke, a machete in hand, and Duke spun, the big blade sailing harmlessly as he slid in next to his attacker, elbow breaking the man's nose even as Duke stepped toward the third attacker. A flurry of punches and the third man went down hard and fast.

The fourth man lunged at Benitez, the medic sidestepping the guy's knife as the doc threw a short, hard right that caught the attacker on the point of the chin and knocked him cold.

Duke shot the medic a questioning glance.

"Golden Gloves," Benitez said, flashing his big smile. "I didn't make your team strictly 'cause I know my way around an aspirin."

Duke returned the smile, then swiveled to see Stearns and Bergman cleaning up their side of the room with the ease of garbage men dumping cans into the back of a truck.

But Ripcord was dealing with the two scantily clad waitresses, each of whom suddenly had knives too, though Duke would never know where the women had them hidden prior to the fight.

The first one came at Rip and he ducked, looping an arm around her so he could come up behind her, using her as a shield against the other. She kicked and screamed.

The second waitress lunged from behind just as Rip spun, the first one still in front of him. The second woman's knife jammed into her friend's shoulder and both their eyes went wide; the first one abruptly stopped her kicking and screaming as she collapsed into Ripcord's arms, fainting apparently at the sight of the blood leaking out of her.

Letting her slide to the floor, Rip turned his attention to the other woman, her face full of stunned anger as she rushed him.

Duke looked over to see the bartender yelling into a cellphone as he pulled a sawed-off shotgun from under the bar.

Ripcord was working out whether he wanted to hit a woman when a flying bottle crashed against her head and dropped her to the floor, unconscious, next to her wounded friend.

As the barkeep's shotgun came up, aimed in the general direction of Ripcord, Duke picked a bottle off a table and flung the missile, connecting squarely with the bartender's jaw, the man's shotgun firing harmlessly if noisily into the air, while the bartender himself dropped to the floor, out cold.

The five would-be mercenaries stood in a tight group, surveying the damage they had wrought on the twenty-five people on the floor, all either unconscious, damaged, or both.

"Almost had to hit a lady," Ripcord said.

Duke said, "That was no lady. Anyway, you knifed the other one."

"No, her *girlfriend* knifed her. I would cop to an assist, though, if you're keeping score."

"Everybody in this joint had a knife," Stearns reminded his teammates.

"Except us," Benitez said.

"Speak for yourself," Bergman said, folding up a switchblade and slipping it into his boot.

"Where'd you get that?" Rip asked. "You flew commercial."

"One of the gentlemen I met tonight insisted I take it from him as a souvenir."

"Threw it at you, you mean," Rip said.

"You got it."

Nodding around the room, Duke said, "Might not be a bad idea for everyone else to grab one too, and I won't complain if everybody picks up a handgun or two."

They quickly searched the bodies and each took a knife. Rip and Stearns wound up with two handguns, Rip's a fairly new automatic, Stearns's a revolver that looked like a relic from the Spanish-American war. As they did this, Benitez made the rounds among the fallen and improvised some first aid.

"All right," Duke said, finally. "We better get the hell out of here before the *federales* show."

The quintet walked outside into the darkness.

"Man, it's quiet," Rip said. "What is it they say in the old movies?"

"Too quiet," Duke said, frowning.

And spotlights exploded in front of them. Duke and the others shaded their eyes as they looked up to see three tanks and maybe twenty soldiers with automatic weapons.

"Guess what?" Duke said. "I think we brought knives to a gunfight."

San Marco, San Sebastiao

The warm night suddenly seemed hotter.

The tanks trained spotlights on the five Americans, and the front row of soldiers had their automatic weapons poised to fire.

A uniformed officer stepped forward—a lieutenant in the sand-colored uniform of the San Sebastiaoan army. Face hard, dark eyes glittering, he said, "*Levantan los manos.*"

This was old news—they had raised their hands automatically, confronted by the guns.

"We're already *levantayin'* our *manos,*" Ripcord said.

The officer threw him a look, as did Duke. The lieutenant came over to Rip, gave him a quick, low right to the breadbasket, and Rip suddenly seemed to be bowing before the man.

The Americans came forward a step, with the exception of Duke, who simply said, "No," and the others froze.

"You okay, bro?" Duke asked.

Ripcord had seen the blow coming, and had

rolled with it, tensing his muscles. "No sweat—dickweed here hits like a little girl."

The lieutenant turned away, then swung around sideways in a sort of martial-arts move, firing a boot into Rip's ribs. This time, Rip didn't see it coming, and the kick knocked him on his butt.

Getting up, brushing himself off, Rip said, "On the other hand, he kicks like a mule and I'm pretty sure he speaks English."

The lieutenant turned to Rip and Duke, and—with barely a trace of an accent—said, "Benefits of an Ivy League education."

"All right," Duke said. "Then maybe you can tell us what the hell's up here."

"*Sí,*" the officer said. "I am Lieutenant Rodolfo Hernandez and what is 'up' here is that my men are about to shoot you as spies."

"Whoa," Duke said, "on what grounds?"

Even with a pistol in his waistband and a knife in his sock, Ripcord felt a little uneasy, looking down the barrels of all these guns. Was Lieutenant Hernandez fishing, or had their cover been blown so quickly? And if so, how?

For now, Rip figured that the best thing was to sit back and let Duke take the lead. For once, he could see the wisdom in keeping his trap shut.

Hernandez waved several soldiers toward the bar. Ripcord immediately started planning exactly which of the San Sebastiaoan soldiers he would take down, if this turned into some kind of Alamo deal. He had Lieutenant Hernandez picked as target number one.

Duke asked, "Just who the hell do you figure we're spying for?"

Hernandez half smiled. "That's the beauty of it—I do not know and I do not care."

"Why would you even *think* we're spies?"

"Anonymous tip."

"You'd kill us on something that thin?"

A full smile blossomed now. "Certainly. These are troubled times, and extreme measures are called for."

Rip watched Duke as his friend processed all the possibilities.

"So the bartender called you," Duke said. "I saw him on his cell."

"Who it was," Hernandez said, "is of no consequence."

"We have a right to confront our accuser."

"No, you don't," Hernandez said with a hearty laugh. "You are not in the United States. This is San Sebastiao. You *have* no rights."

"San Sebastiao," Duke said, "is a democratic country and a friend of the United States. We have an embassy—I demand—"

Hernandez cut Duke off with another laugh, but the laugh itself was interrupted by a voice from the darkness saying: "We *are* a democracy and a friend of the U.S.—but we are a sovereign nation as well."

They turned toward the voice and a curly-haired man in an elaborately medal-adorned army uniform stepped out into the glare of the floodlights.

Hernandez damn near fainted. *"Atención!"* he barked.

Twenty men snapped to as the high-ranking officer walked farther into the light. Even before anyone said anything, Ripcord recognized a prominent face from the briefing: *General Pedro Lopez himself*.

As if to confirm Rip's ID, Hernandez said, "General Lopez," and saluted smartly.

The general had shiny epaulets with enough stars on his shoulders to crowd the sky, and gold braid on his cap, shoulders, and sleeves—plus enough lettuce on his chest to make a salad that could feed his whole army.

Rip wondered about that—San Sebastiao's only war had been a brief border skirmish with Colombia, some time ago. Where had the general earned all these campaign ribbons making such a colorful puzzle on his left breast?

In English, Lopez said, "Lieutenant, have you checked their papers?"

The junior officer shook his head, a rebuked child. He clearly knew he was waist deep in brown water, and led the general a few steps away, where the two men conferred just out of Rip and Duke's earshot.

After the conversation, Lopez came back to the five members of the team. "You may put your hands down, gentlemen."

They did as they were told, Rip preparing himself to jerk the pistol out of his back waistband and grab the general as a hostage. He needed only a couple of steps to be close enough. . . .

"Your papers?" General Lopez asked, looking at Duke.

Duke complied, and the rest followed suit. Rip knew their papers were perfect, could pass any test. In San Sebastiao, he was not Wallace Weems, but Darius Jackson, an ex-Marine with skills strangely like those of Wallace Weems. What troubled Rip, at the moment, were the soldiers in the bar—they had been gone for quite a while now.

"Richard Bolden," Lopez read aloud. "Jaime, come!"

A slender, middle-aged major emerged from the darkness, a laptop computer under his arm.

"This is my assistant," Lopez said with a nod to the newcomer. "Jaime, find out about Mr. Bolden."

Taking the papers from the general, Jaime set the laptop on the trunk of a nearby parked car and started tapping keys.

After a moment, the major said, "Richard James Bolden, former U.S. Marine. Paratrooper, attained the rank of captain, was demoted to sergeant before his dishonorable discharge."

Frowning, Duke demanded, "How did he *do* that? My record was sealed when the Marines booted me!"

Lopez smiled. "All locked doors can be unlocked, Mr. Bolden, if one only has the right key. If I may, why the demotion?"

Duke shrugged. "I punched out a superior officer."

"And why would you do such a thing?"

"The S.O.B. got my men killed on a mission."

The major at the laptop chimed in: "That was in the Middle East, General!"

Lopez considered that for a long moment. Shortly,

a soldier exited the bar and came over to whisper something in the general's ear.

Rip moved two steps closer to Lopez and let his right hand drift to his right hip. *If this was going down, it was going down soon. . . .*

Returning to Duke, Lopez—his eyes on the front door of the cantina—said, "You men stirred up a good deal of trouble in there."

"We didn't stir up anything," Duke said. "What we did was strictly self-defense. Our medical guy even patched up some of the wounded."

"Some of the *twenty-five* you wounded?"

"Twenty-six with the bartender," Duke said, "is my count. But math isn't my greatest skill."

"Are you sure? I would think you'd count subtraction as among your best attributes." Shaking his head, the general said, "Three were *severely* wounded. An ambulance is on the way."

But the ambulance, obviously, was not as fast as the military in this city.

Rip stepped forward. "That waitress got stabbed by the *other* waitress—wasn't us."

"So," Lopez said, almost cheerfully, "you are only responsible for twenty-five of the casualties in the cantina."

"Sounds about right," Duke said.

"Two dozen citizens is one thing," Lopez said. "But the army? That is quite another. Surely you do not intend to cause any further fuss? There are twenty men and three tanks."

Duke said nothing.

Taking a different tack, Lopez said, "Lieutenant

Hernandez apparently acted in haste. You are guests in our country, and you deserve a hearing."

"Is that what we're going to get? A hearing?"

"No. You have already had that. I have made up my mind about you gentlemen. Because you do have . . . certain . . . *skills.*"

"That we do."

"And what are you talented individuals doing, now that you are not in the Marines any longer?"

Duke shrugged. "When we separated from the Marine Corps, we decided we liked our jobs, just not our employer. So, you could say that we have maintained the same skill set—we're just looking for a new boss."

Lopez stroked his chin, and his smile was sly. "Tell me—what brings you to our sunny country?"

"Rumor has it there's a not-so-sunny civil war going on. And where there are two armies fighting, one side or the other is generally looking for help."

"And it matters not which side pays?"

Shaking his head, Duke said, "Not in the least. You pay, we play—that's our motto."

"Which makes it rather difficult for one to trust you, then—doesn't it?"

Duke shook his head again. "Once we take on a job, we take it on. We're professionals, and if word got out that we weren't loyal to our employers, who would hire us?"

"Ah, but word never gets out, when no one is left behind to talk."

Duke locked eyes with Lopez. "Trust runs both ways, General. If you don't trust us, you can damn well bet we won't be trusting you. No commercial enterprise does well without trust on *both* sides . . . and that includes war."

"The biggest commercial enterprise of them all," Lopez said, nodding. "If I had some work, Mr. Bolden, that might have need of your team's skills—would you be interested?"

"I don't know enough to say yes or no," Duke said. "But I am willing to listen. We made a long trip for that very opportunity."

Lopez damn near beamed. He gestured grandly. "Well, then, gentlemen—why don't we provide you some transportation to the presidential palace? We can talk more there."

"Sounds like a plan," Duke said.

General Lopez nodded to his assistant.

"*Inmediatamente,* sir," Jaime said, and started talking to Lieutenant Hernandez beyond the team's hearing.

"Satisfy my curiosity," Lopez said to Duke, his tone conversational now. "How did you think you would get out of here with just the five of you?"

With a nod toward Rip, Duke said, "The man next to you has a pistol in his waistband. He would have taken you hostage."

Rip gave the general a look at the pistol in his rear waistband.

"Then," Duke said, "the rest of my men would have got into it."

"The rest?" Lopez asked.

Duke whistled and four men came out of hiding places around the street.

"Even though you outnumber us, and have superior weapons," Duke said, "we would have had you in a cross fire. It might have proved an interesting exercise."

There were now nine members of Duke's team surrounding the general.

Genuinely impressed, the general was about to say something to Duke when the squat sniper, Ray Peters, trotted up to join them.

"A *tenth* man?" the general asked, eyebrows up as if in surrender.

"Sorry," Peters said to Duke. "I was in the bell tower of the church up the street. There's no elevator."

The general turned to Duke and shook his hand. "I think we're going to be good friends, Mr. Bolden. Very good friends indeed. You have a lovely sense of stealth."

Duke grinned back. "I like the sound of that, sir."

From his position atop a nearby building, in his hooded black ninja attire, Snake Eyes watched the general's Humvee pull away, a truck loaded with the American team behind it, the three tanks, and a truck bearing the platoon of infantry men after that.

This was part of the Americans' plan, to infiltrate General Lopez's army as mercenaries. So far, their scheme seemed to be playing out—unless, of course, they were being hauled away to be executed.

That didn't seem to be the case, however, as the general and the team leader had been smiling and occasionally even laughing when the team climbed into the back of the truck. The San Sebastiaoan army did not seem to be treating the Americans as prisoners at all.

The building where Snake Eyes was set up had been his second choice: The bell tower of the church would have been his first, but the U.S. team's sniper had gotten there before him and— given General Hawk's directive that they not interact with them—Snake Eyes had deferred to the American, and found another spot down the street.

Settling for his second choice, though, had given Snake Eyes a faster route to the street. Instead of going down the inside of the building, when the convoy started to move, he vaulted over onto the next roof, a structure a story shorter than his original post, and somersaulted to protect himself as he landed.

After sprinting across the rooftop, he launched his body and caught the gutter of the next one, shimmying down the drainpipe till he hung just above roof level of the next building over. Bracing his feet against the wall, Snake Eyes pushed himself backward, until the drainpipe gave way, sagging from its building over toward its next-door neighbor, Snake Eyes dropping onto that roof.

He peeked over the edge and saw what he wanted: The convoy was on this street, headed his way. In the darkness, he could jump from this roof onto the top of a passing vehicle and, with any luck, not be heard or seen.

Timing it out, Snake Eyes made his move, dropping onto the middle of the three tanks in line. With another tank both in front and behind him, the darkness made it difficult for anyone in either truck to see him, and also gave him a thick, metallic surface to drop onto. When he hit, he froze, hanging on and waiting for the hatch to open, if someone inside had heard him. Seconds passed and, finally, he decided his entrance had gone undetected.

A curfew had been enforced since the death of President Vicente and these streets were—but for the occasional military vehicle—deserted, as the convoy rolled through the capital city. As he stowed away atop the tank, pressed flat to avoid detection, Snake Eyes used his wrist communicator to text a coded message to Gung Ho. The note was terse, informing his team leader what had happened and where they were headed.

Snake Eyes didn't know a lot about the geography of San Marco, but he figured eventually this convoy would end up at the presidential palace. The question he had for his unit leader was whether or not to ride the convoy all the way in or not.

The message back from Gung Ho required no use of code: *Be careful.*

As the convoy rolled past the building where the rest of his G.I. JOE unit was holed up for the night, Snake Eyes thought he caught a glimpse of Scarlett in a window. Probably just his imagination . . . or perhaps wishful thinking. . . .

The convoy went through the palace gates without anyone spotting Snake Eyes, and—as soon as the tanks veered off the main drive into one of the darker sections of the grounds—he beat a hasty exit from his armored taxi and disappeared on foot, into the night.

Running, keeping low, hidden by the shadows, Snake Eyes made his way to a tree only twenty yards from the front entrance of the presidential palace.

He watched the American team climb down from the truck, standing around outside with their new friend, General Lopez, who had come back from his Humvee. The leader of the American team, Hauser, spoke with the general briefly; and then the team entered the palace, seemingly on the best of terms with Lopez.

Snake Eyes wanted a closer look, and knew he could infiltrate the palace with little trouble. But if he ran into any unfriendlies—and had to deal with them—the Able Team's covers would likely be blown. And he would have single-handedly screwed over the Americans, and endangered the G.I. JOE unit's mission as well.

For now, it was enough to know that the Americans seemed to be proceeding safely on their mission, and that the JOEs' parallel mission could move forward without interfering with Able Team.

Best just to leave, for now.

Getting out would be easier than getting in—the security in places like this, after all, was designed to keep intruders out, not keep them in once they'd gotten there.

Even on foot, in a city he did not know, Snake Eyes had rejoined the JOEs in their safe house well before dawn.

*   *   *

For the past two hours, Able Team had been wined and dined as if they were the guests of honor at a state dinner—turkey, chicken, ham, prime rib, salmon, anything they wanted to eat or drink was lavishly served by a staff decked out in black slacks and white tuxedo shirts with bow ties, not unlike back at Tom and Harvey's in D.C.

Though the general at the head of the banquet table was eating and drinking like just another one of the guys, Duke figured Lopez was keeping them busy while his people did further research into the team's legends, as the CIA put it.

That the banquet was still going on told Duke their covers were holding up to the scrutiny of Lopez's assistant, Major Jaime, and Jaime's staff.

As if on cue, Jaime strolled into the room and up to the head of the table, where he stopped and spoke in General Lopez's ear. The general bestowed a small grin and nodded, prompting the major to stand behind him to one side.

"Well," Duke said genially. "Are we who we say we are?"

General Lopez's smile widened. "Why ask me that now, Mr. Bolden?"

Duke's smile matched the general's in wattage. "Because your people have had time by now to visit my mother and ask to see my birth certificate."

Lopez chuckled. "And what makes you think we didn't?"

Rip said, "If you fellas talked to *my* mama, I hope you told her her favorite son is eatin' high on the hog."

The general's smile hardened. "Ah, Mr. Jackson. Your file indicates you have an inclination toward playing the fool. But would you prefer to make jokes . . . or talk business?"

Ripcord shrugged. "Hey, I can multitask. Talk business with my boy Bolden here, and I'll toss in the quip now and then, no extra charge."

Lopez just stared at Rip, apparently trying to decide if he could take this joker seriously or not.

"*I'm* here to talk *business*," Duke said, amping his voice up some, trying to break the tension between Lopez and Rip. "Do you have a job for us?"

Lopez returned his attention to Duke. "Yes, Mr. Bolden—a very important job, in fact . . . I want you to kill someone."

He might have said, "I want you to pick up a package at the post office."

After trading a look with Rip, Duke asked, "Just one?"

Lopez kept his voice light. "Isn't killing people a large part of what you do?"

"Well," Duke said, "certainly that comes into play—we're a military-style team."

"Which kills people."

"Yeah, but usually not one at a time. Isn't it kind of overkill, so many men with guns and just one target?"

"A military team," Lopez said, "is exactly what this particular mission calls for."

Rip said, "To kill one man."

Lopez lowered his eyes but lifted a forefinger. "One man . . . guarded by many."

"Okay," Duke said. "Who's the target?"

His face expressionless, his voice light, Lopez said, "Jose Ansalmo—vice president of San Sebastiao."

Silence draped the dining hall.

Then Duke said, "Political assassinations are expensive, General. Anybody involved knows the survival rate of assassination squads is dismal."

"You will be well paid, and you will be escorted safely out of the country."

"Your vice president," Duke said, as if tasting the words. "I'm not exactly a geopolitical whiz, but I heard he disappeared. It was on *Fox News* and everything."

Lopez had a distant smile, as if recalling an amusing anecdote. "That is the . . . *public* face of it. The truth is, Ansalmo is in hiding."

"I see." Duke sipped a glass of beer. "Do we know *where* he's hiding?"

"Certainly—in a monastery thirty kilometers from the city."

"If you know where he is," Rip said, "why don't you send your soldiers out there and kill the damn fool?"

"A reasonable question, Mr. Jackson. The problem is, not only is Ansalmo first in the line of succession to President Vicente, he is also a very popular political figure in his own right."

"So," Duke said, "you can't be seen as responsible."

The general's smile and his shrug conveyed: *What's a man to do?* Then he said: "If my men were tied to his murder, the rebellion would intensify."

"But on the other hand," Duke said, "if the *rebels* seem to be behind the assassination . . . ?"

Lopez smiled big. "Astute, Mr. Bolden. In that case, the people will support the head of the military in taking over and putting a stop to the civil war."

"In other words, you'd be the Man," Rip said.

Lopez bobbed his head in a sort of bow.

"You'd have nearly unlimited power," Duke said, admiringly.

Lopez waved that off. "The most important thing is to bring peace to our great country. Law and order needs to be restored, gentlemen, even if it means a temporary suspension of democratic government and certain privileges."

"Of course," Duke said wryly. "Peace is always the overriding concern."

Lopez frowned, just a little. "Mr. Bolden, your tone is mocking—do you question my motives?"

"No, General. That's not my prerogative. While it's gratifying to feel we're on the side of right, our only real concern is money."

Lopez clapped his hands together and laughed, once. "That is very good, Mr. Bolden. Very humorous. I admire your way of thinking. Am I right in saying we have reached an accord?"

"Not yet, we haven't, General . . . but you're getting warmer."

The general studied his guest. "Ah, the precise amount—how does this sound—ten million *pesetas* . . . each?"

Duke took a moment to make the mental calculations on the exchange rate, which meant about

$750,000 apiece for the members of his team. (He had lied about his math skills.)

"General," Duke said with a grin, "it sounds *muy bueno* to me, with—"

"*Maravilloso,*" Lopez said.

Duke said, "You didn't let me finish. I was starting to say, 'with one exception. . . .' Make it *dollars,* not *pesetas.*"

Lopez eyed Duke for a long time. "We will make it, say, twelve million *pesetas.*"

Nine hundred thousand apiece. Better, but still too low.

Duke said, "General, your country is in the midst of a civil war. Let's agree first that the payment will be in dollars. The *peseta* is an unstable currency right now. Make it two million American dollars per man."

Lopez seemed to squirm a bit. "Dollars, agreed . . . but two million each is outright theft."

"Outright theft offends you?" Duke asked. "When you're asking us to commit murder?"

"*You're* asking for twenty million dollars."

"Too much to bring peace to your *oil-rich* country?" Duke asked.

He couldn't seem to give in too easily. Lopez needed to believe they were real mercenaries, which meant tough negotiating for the best deal.

Lopez gave up a little shrug. "Not too much for what I want—just more than we have available right now."

"What *can* you afford?" Duke asked.

Lopez considered that. "My administration's costs are high, and getting higher by the day. We've had to import certain . . . *tools* for this undertaking, which has had a bigger impact on our budget than anticipated. But I am in a unique position to make you a one-of-a-kind proposition, Mr. Bolden."

"I'm listening."

"Let us say one million American dollars per man"—the general's eyes narrowed and his smile was a perverted thing—"and I will make *each* of you generals in the new army I will soon assemble."

"What kind of cut-rate coup are you running here? Half-price, and we get to nursemaid a bunch of new recruits afterward? I don't think so, General."

Raising his palms in a placating manner, Lopez said, "The money will be in cash, and the army will *not* be new recruits. Well, not *exactly* new recruits. . . ."

"That doesn't sound enticing in the least."

But Lopez was warming to his subject: "Your men fight for money—*my* men out of patriotism or a loyalty to me, if not to country . . . but all have one thing in common."

"Which is?"

"Fear."

"Fear?"

He nodded. "Even the bravest of the brave, like yourself, Mr. Bolden, and your comrades. No matter how good you are as soldiers, you still feel fear. Oh, the best—like you—can control it; but it still is part of your human makeup, and your decision-making process."

The general leaned forward, as if sharing a very terrible secret—and perhaps he was.

"Imagine, Mr. Bolden," Lopez said, his voice as hushed as if in church, "soldiers *without* fear."

"I've got one next to me," Duke said, jerking a thumb at Rip.

Lopez shook his head. "I don't mean *bravado*, Mr. Bolden—I mean literally, a fighting man who feels *no* fear."

Duke grunted a skeptical laugh. "Impossible."

But Lopez shook his head again, even more emphatically. "No, sir. It may seem improbable, but my importer says there is a scientist as brilliant as Einstein himself working in a secure laboratory, focused on overcoming that very problem . . . *right* now."

"Never happen," Duke said.

Lopez shrugged. "That was my initial assessment as well. Then I saw a video of the research. It's not perfected yet, but the answer is near . . . very near. When I am able to build an army of such super soldiers, I will need highly trained, *highly paid* commanders. Those commanders could be *your* team, Mr. Bolden."

"Let me see the video, and maybe we'll talk."

The general made a noncommittal shrug. "Impossible, I'm afraid."

"Gotta see it," Duke said, shaking his head in matter-of-fact skepticism. "Make us believe the super soldier thing is possible, and you have a deal. Being a well-paid general in a warm-weather country, with no extradition agreement with the U.S., well, that sounds like it could be a good gig."

"Gig?"

"Job."

Lopez grinned. He turned to the major, just behind him. "Jaime, bring *Señor* Chernitz and tell him to bring the DVD."

"Sí, mi general."

The major left and Lopez and his guests were enjoying some wine when Jaime returned with a tall, bearded man, not Hispanic, in a blue silk shirt and Levi's. An American maybe, but there was something about him that made Duke think Eastern European. He carried a small black DVD case.

Chernitz eyeballed Duke and his men. The "importer" obviously had at least some idea why he was there.

"General, are you sure you want to share this with . . . your, uh, guests?"

Duke recognized the accent as Eastern European, possibly even Uzekurki—not likely a coincidence, after their last mission. . . .

Rising, Lopez took the DVD from Chernitz. "Emile, these men are not just guests—they are about to become patriots in our cause."

Chernitz appeared unimpressed—he had probably seen more than his share of mercenaries.

"These men will be the generals of my new army," the general went on, enthusiastically. "It's only fitting that they should get a preview of the kind of army they will be leading."

Lopez handed the disc to Jaime, who went to a player on a wall shelf; another wall, the one Duke and Rip were facing, was quickly home to a big screen that dropped down.

Soon they were watching video of a soldier in camo-fatigues standing against a concrete wall, an M16 in his hands; a smaller wall, about three feet high and four feet wide, was to one side of him.

Then the view switched from front to side shot, revealing the soldier facing another man in fatigues who pointed a handgun at him, a .45. A graphic came up in the corner indicating a date three weeks earlier; beneath that: TRIAL SEVEN.

When the graphic disappeared, the man with the .45 began firing shots at the man with the M16, bullets ricocheting off the concrete wall around him. Duke was reminded of the circus stunt where a knife thrower hurled blades at an unflinching woman standing against a backboard.

But these were bullets, cement dust and chunks flying, and still the soldier never moved. When the man with the handgun had emptied the clip, he re-loaded and the man against the wall remained mo-tionless as the second clip was emptied around him.

Halfway through a third clip, a scarlet puff erupted next to the man with the M16, his arm badly pierced. And yet he responded not at all.

The screen went to black.

"Is that real?" Duke asked Chernitz.

"Yes," he said.

Ripcord was wincing like he was the one who had had his arm shot by a .45. "Why the hell didn't that idiot move?"

"Or take cover," Duke asked, "and shoot back?"

Chernitz said, "The chemical cocktail intended

to dull the fight-or-flight instinct of the soldier was actually too strong, thwarting his fight instinct. So, instead of ducking behind the low wall and returning fire, he simply stood there, even after being wounded."

"So," Rip said, frowning in thought, "it's just a matter of getting the dosage right?"

"Yes. But when we do, we will revolutionize warfare—as you can see, not only was fear suppressed, the man felt no pain. But there are still bugs to work out."

"Bugs?" Duke asked.

"Well, the test subjects have exhibited suicidal tendencies after two weeks on the mixture. So that needs to be worked out as well."

"All right," Duke said, and let out a breath. "This is obviously a serious breakthrough. The possibility of 'super soldiers' is no pipe dream. . . . You have a deal, General."

Lopez beamed. "You show excellent judgment, Mr. Bolden."

"Thanks," Duke said. "Now, it's time for you to bring us up to speed on the target."

Chernitz retrieved his DVD and retired. The general's assistant plugged his laptop into the projector and brought up a map of San Marco and the surrounding area.

Standing near the screen, Lopez pointed out a spot on the map northeast of the city. "Thirty kilometers from the capital is a monastery known as the Brotherhood of the Servants of Santa Maria. This is where the coward Ansalmo is hiding."

"I take it security is considerable?" Duke asked.

"At least twenty armed men. Members of the *Guardia Nacional.*"

"Good men?"

"They're not professional soldiers," Lopez said, cocking his head, "but most have had *some* military training, and they're *all* policemen . . . so they should not be underestimated."

"Which is why," Duke said, "you weren't looking for the proverbial lone gunman."

Lopez nodded. "Ansalmo probably has a platoon's worth of men guarding him."

"Who's in charge?"

"Roberto Romero—head of the *Guardia Nacional,* and also Ansalmo's brother-in-law. He would give his life for Ansalmo, this I know for a certainty. To kill one, you will have to kill the other. And you have my blessing to do so."

Duke nodded. "What kind of weapons?"

"They will have AK–47s—beyond that, I don't know."

"What about the monastery itself?"

"Built before the Quichans were converted to Catholicism—therefore, a walled fortress. Three buildings inside—a barn and granary that the monks use for sustenance, a chapel, and the monks' living quarters."

"And Ansalmo and his bodyguards are bunking with the monks?"

"*Si,*" Lopez said.

"Do you want us to avoid bloodshed where the monks are concerned? Are we talking surgical strike?"

The general thought about that for a moment.

"Don't worry about sending the monks to their precious heaven. They are mere collateral damage, and we will blame their deaths on the rebels, in any case. Their deaths by violence may be useful for propaganda purposes, so do not be bashful, gentlemen."

Duke nodded. "We'll need a truck. And in the morning, I'll give you a list of other supplies. For now? We need rest."

"Would you like to stay here?" the general asked. "You would have guest rooms, not barracks."

Duke shook his head. "We'll go back to our hotels and be back at noon tomorrow."

"How much planning will be needed?"

"I've already started. This is going to be a night operation . . . and the sooner we go, the better."

"What if I was to insist on being part of that planning?" Lopez asked, his voice slightly colder.

"Then we've got a problem," Duke said, "and you can find yourself another hit team—you're the boss, all right. But we don't go to work for you until noon tomorrow. Until then, this is my team and we need to have a conference—alone."

Lopez shrugged and found a smile for them. "I will not question your way of doing things, Mr. Bolden."

"Same back at you."

"Then, tomorrow you will do the job?"

"No point in putting it off," Duke said. "Like you said, General, why be bashful?"

CHAPTER SEVEN
Monklike Existence

San Sebastiao

Duke had given Lopez a fairly simple list of equipment and supplies, which the general had easily filled. Each man had an M16 (with the exception of Bergman, who carried a heavier M–60), a Glock with noise suppressor, a combat knife, three hand grenades, a canteen, night-vision goggles, and a communicator system that consisted of a wrist-mic and earpiece.

To Ripcord's pleasure, the officer assigned to oversee their outfitting was Lieutenant Hernandez, who had kicked Rip the night before. Whether the lieutenant being there was a coincidence or a gift from General Lopez, Rip had no way of knowing; but he would damn sure take advantage of it. . . .

When they were outfitted and ready, Rip went up to Hernandez and the officer's eyes burned into Rip's in a Latin cocktail of hate and shame. They stood almost nose to nose, the stare down lasting nearly half a minute before Duke put a hand on Rip's arm and gave him a "Let's go" head shake.

Rip nodded. "Oh, one other thing I need," he said, spinning suddenly, his boot coming up and connecting with the lieutenant's midsection, lifting him off the ground and doubling him over, then depositing him in a rude sitting position on the gravel.

"I can't take you anywhere," Duke said to Rip.

General Lopez hurried over to see what was going on, but in what was likely a testament to Hernandez's lack of popularity with his own men, no one took so much as a step toward the American and his comrades.

Lopez demanded, "What is the idea of assaulting my lieutenant?"

Ripcord shrugged. "Lieutenant Hernandez and me, we got off on the wrong foot last night. Just setting that straight."

Lopez said nothing, but his eyes were unhappy.

"We need to get moving," Duke told the general.

"Godspeed," Lopez said, which Rip found an interesting send-off, considering they were about to raid a monastery.

The truck took them only partway—Duke hadn't wanted to announce their presence, so the vehicle had parked off the side of a rutted dirt road ten klicks from their destination. From there, they hoofed it.

Ripcord found himself on point again, but this time—instead of the frigid winter of Uzekurkistan—they were trudging through the humid San Sebastiaoan jungle. No white parka for Rip this time—sweat drenched his camouflage fatigues.

No bullets whizzed around his head, but mosquitoes the size of hummingbirds did, strafing the team, sucking enough blood to rival a firefight.

In his earpiece, Rip heard Duke ask, "How's it goin' up there, bro?"

"Walk in the park, so far," Rip said. "Admit I was tempted to hop the back of one of these skeeters and just fly along. How do you like ridin' drag, son?"

"Nice and quiet back here, without you yammering. You seein' anything up there?"

"No," Rip said, not liking the tone of his friend's voice. "Your Spidey sense tinglin' or somethin'?"

". . . I don't think we're alone."

"Maybe it's Jesus, lookin' out for those monks."

A moment's hesitation preceded Duke saying, "Could be Lopez double-crossing us. Could also be the rebels."

"Maybe your conscience finally caught up with you," Rip said.

". . . I just know somebody's out there."

Duke had gone from thinking somebody was trailing them to knowing. That, Rip felt, was worth taking seriously.

But he asked, "Based on what, bro?"

"My gut."

"When's the last time you ate?"

Duke said, "Breakfast."

"So are we talkin' intuition or growlin' stomach?"

"Either way, keep your eyes open up there. I'm telling you, buddy . . . somebody's in this jungle with us, and I don't mean Tarzan."

*   *   *

The undergrowth was thick as anything Gung Ho had ever encountered, even on snake hunts along the Bayou Teche, back home in Louisiana.

Still, they were making good time, the five JOEs moving more easily through the heavily wooded area than the U.S. military team moving parallel to them, five hundred yards to the east.

The G.I. JOE team tried to keep the Americans slightly ahead, so Unit Alpha could guard Able Team's back. Gung Ho figured the American team leader, Hauser, surely suspected a possible double-cross; but the JOE leader was certain of it.

They had left behind Joaquin and Antonia, their Quichan guides, to begin trailing the American team. An hour or so in, Joaquin had radioed that General Lopez and a sizable force were moving out from the palace and heading in the same direction as the Americans.

At once, Gung Ho had fathomed the general's plan. Though the primary JOE objective was to keep the pulse weapons out of the rebels' hands, the secondary one was to provide clandestine support to the American team . . . and, right now, Gung Ho considered that the priority. . . .

The rebels had been uncharacteristically quiet since the assassination of President Vicente. This indicated that the rebels did not have the pulse weapons. Now if *Lopez* had the next-gen weapons, the general would most likely keep them on the down low, till the heat over the president's assassination cooled. In that case, Gung Ho knew, General Lopez would be looking for plausible deniability.

His wrist communicator vibrated—a coded message from Snake Eyes. As usual, the ninja was traveling solo, currently scouting the position, and progress, of the U.S. team.

Decoded, the message read, *Five klicks to go—so far so good.*

If Gung Ho was right about Lopez's plan, and he had no doubt otherwise, "so far so good" would maybe be another five klicks . . . then all hell would break loose.

"Yo, JOEs—let's hustle up!"

In the back of his Humvee, speeding up the road in the company of Emile Chernitz, General Pedro Lopez felt good about himself. In front were the driver and Major Jaime, using GPS to track the mercenaries' truck. A transport of San Sebastiaoan soldiers followed, with two tanks farther back.

Everything was falling into place for Lopez—before dawn, he would have what he wanted, what he needed. The only thing standing in the way of complete control of the country was that self-righteous fool, Ansalmo.

Lopez could never feel truly in command while the popular, people's choice vice president still breathed God's air. As per plan, the populace for the most part believed the rebels had killed *Presidente* Vicente. If the rebels took the blame for killing *both* the president and vice president, the path would be clear for strong leader Lopez taking over, with a mandate for quelling the rebellion, and bringing the killers of Vicente and Ansalmo to justice. Such could make Lopez the same kind of life-long leader as his childhood hero, Fidel Castro.

"Sir," Jaime said, "GPS indicates we're coming up to the truck. . . ."

That pleased Lopez—the soldiers of fortune he had hired knew their deadly business. They had better sense than to drive all the way to the monastery, though the mercenaries had, in fact, stopped even sooner than Lopez might have expected. . . .

"Perhaps you should send out a patrol," Chernitz said, somewhat nervously.

Lopez managed to not laugh out loud at the craven arms dealer—his contempt for whom remained a concealed weapon, for now. The general still needed the man and his pulse rifles . . . and, more important, in days ahead, the so-called super soldiers this coward could provide.

"No," Lopez said. "It will be fine. The mercenaries are long gone. They are marching in."

"You're *sure* of this?"

Spreading his hands, Lopez said, "What does it matter? Even if they left a man behind, to guard the truck? He can die now as easily as later."

That remark seemed to surprise, even shock, Chernitz. The gunrunner—despite all the death he'd sold to the highest bidder—was really quite squeamish about killing close at hand.

And indeed people were going to die tonight—many people.

Lopez had been developing the plan from the moment Ansalmo had escaped an assassination attempt set for the same day as the president's killing.

But Ansalmo had suspected something, and his man Romero had sneaked him out past Lopez's assassins and their pulse rifles.

Since Ansalmo had outsmarted him and gone into hiding, Lopez had considered manufacturing evidence to feed to the press, implicating the vice president in the plot to kill Vicente. That plan, however, was complicated and would have been difficult to carry out, requiring numerous conspirators. This new plan, however, was beautiful in its simplicity.

The mercenaries would kill Ansalmo and, undoubtedly, most of his security force. Lopez and his men would arrive at the monastery in an attempt to "save" the vice president, but would show up too late to save Ansalmo himself, though just in time to supply rough, immediate justice to the assassination team.

Not long afterward, Lopez would provide the press information linking the mercenaries to the rebels. That the mercenaries were Americans would be an unexpected plus, helping him whip his citizens into a fury against the United States. In the end, they would support anything he did, including nationalizing the oil industry and kicking out the American oil companies.

With the government under his control, and nationalized oil giving him a major source of revenue, *Generalísimo* Pedro Lopez would spend the rest of his life living like a king—a king with an army of super soldiers armed with pulse rifles. Over the next ten years, he would see his country's borders expand like a prosperous man's waistline.

Yes, already he was daring to dream that his tiny country would grow ever larger, swallowing up its neighbors on a path to complete control of South America. He would be the ruler of a country that could rival any superpower, the United States included; and for that to happen, the sacrifice of a few people, innocent monks among them, was a ridiculously small price to pay.

The Humvee took a left onto a dirt path.

"Where are you *going*?" Lopez demanded of the driver. "Jaime, I thought you said we were getting close!"

"They pulled off the road, *mi general*. It is off this way, somewhere."

They bumped and bounced a hundred yards down the rutted path into the jungle. After coming around a bend, the driver stomped the brakes. Chernitz and Lopez both had to brace themselves to keep from hurtling into the back of the driver and passenger seats. Lopez was about to bark a rebuke when through the windshield loomed the truck, parked not ten yards ahead.

To the vehicle hauling soldiers behind them, Lopez yelled, "Check it out!"

The transport stopped, ten men poured out, and they went to investigate the apparently abandoned truck.

Soon Lieutenant Hernandez, in sunglasses despite the deep shade of the jungle, came to the window of the Humvee.

"It is empty, *mi general*."

Nodding, Lopez said, "Back to the road. We'll

circle and catch up with them at the monastery. No use us tromping through the jungle, too."

"*Sí, mi general,*" Hernandez said, then he ordered his men back to their transport.

"One more thing!" Lopez called, an afterthought.

"*Sí, mi general?*"

"Disable that vehicle. Pull the rotor. I want them to think it is all right, should by some miracle they make it back this far."

"*Sí, mi general,*" Hernandez said and did as he was told.

Chernitz—sweating profusely, his face an even pastier white than usual—looked as though the bumpy ride had made him carsick.

"Cheer up, Emile," Lopez said. "Things are unfolding perfectly. Everything according to plan."

Chernitz lifted a skeptical eyebrow. "Everything looked good the day *Vicente* was shot, too. Yet, here we are in the jungle today, still chasing Ansalmo."

Lopez said nothing as the Humvee, with nowhere to turn around, lurched backward; they would have to back all the way to the highway. This gave Lopez longer to think about whether he could still acquire the pulse rifles and the super soldiers, if he gave in to himself and killed this cowardly *maricón* in the seat beside him.

Able Team had found a spot on a hill above and behind the monastery.

They were secluded in the trees, ghosts with infrared vision looking down into the monastery in the darkness. Though midnight neared, and the San Sebastiao nights reportedly were cool, Duke still had sweat pouring off him. The humidity never let up, pressing down on them like clammy hands. Nearly as annoying were the mosquitoes, which dive-bombed the team constantly, mini-vampires impervious to repellent, sucking blood and leaving behind huge red welts and vicious itching.

The team was fanned out across the hill, lying low, Duke and Ripcord in position to see the whole layout from their spot halfway up a banyan tree.

"A gate on the opposite side, in front," Duke said. "A single door back here. Built to be easily defended."

"Two guards on each exit, one on each wall, two rovers," Rip said, his voice low. "They're not exactly expecting trouble."

"Hard to get in, though," Duke said.

"Yeah, and hard to get out, in a pinch."

"Which is why Lopez hired us. He's had Ansalmo blocked in. As long as the V.P. can't get out, he's no real danger to the general. Sooner or later, though, the man's going to make a break for it."

Rip half-grinned. "Suppose we could wait for him."

"They've got livestock, grain, and a well in there. It could be a long freakin' wait."

"Yeah, and anyway, these skeeters will have all the blood drained out of us in an hour or two."

The easy way in would be to shoot the men off the walls, blow the door with grenades, and just storm the damn place. But Duke didn't want to kill any of Ansalmo's bodyguards, not if he could help it, anyway. This made entry into the monastery a little trickier. . . .

As if reading his mind, Rip said, "Don't laugh, but it's a monastery, right? Who says we're not weary travelers looking for rest and religion? In other words, we could walk up and knock on the damn door."

"That might work," Duke allowed, swiftly scanning the monastery again. "It might also kick off a helluva big firefight that would be . . . counterproductive."

"Well, I'm out of genius ideas. Isn't that what they pay *you* for?"

Duke took a long look around the monastery and finally found what he was after. "Yeah, it is . . . and I have one."

"Uh-oh."

"What do you mean, 'uh-oh'?"

"Well, it's just that you've got a plan, and I ain't gonna like it, am I?"

"How do you know? You haven't even heard it yet."

Shifting slightly on his branch, sliding his night-vision goggles up to his forehead, Rip said, "I just know your plan's gonna be a way in without doin' harm to any of the lowlifes in there who'll be doing their best to kill *our* red-white-and-blue butts."

Sliding his own goggles up, Duke said, "Pretty much."

"I vote no."

With a half grin, Duke said, "Good thing we're not a democracy."

"I thought we were bringin' democracy to San Sebastiao?"

"To San Sebastiao. Not to Able Team." Using his wrist communicator, still keeping his voice low, Duke said, "Number three."

"Three here," came Bergman's reply.

"Found yourself some high ground?"

"Roger that."

"Can you see the entire yard?"

Bergman said, "Roger, number one. Can wipe it clean from here."

"Roger that," Duke said. "Soldier, you don't fire except on my order—understood?"

"Roger that, number one."

Rip asked, "What if something happens to you?"

With a rueful smirk, Duke said, "You better make sure it doesn't, or it'll be on your butt."

"Swell," Rip said.

"Number five," Duke said into the communicator.

"Roger five," said the voice of the sniper, Peters.

"You heard what I said to number three?"

"Roger."

"Same order. Found a place?"

"Top of the world."

Duke looked over his shoulder and up the hill. In the darkness, seeing anything but vague shapes was impossible. But even if he'd had searchlights, he still wouldn't have spotted Peters—once the squat sniper had his hiding spot staked out, he was the invisible man.

"Number four," Duke said.

"Roger four," Stearns said.

"On me, now."

"Roger that, one."

"Rest of you," Duke said, "sit tight till you hear from me."

One by one, they all rogered the instruction.

Turning to Rip, he said, "Okay, now—everything hinges on you, bro."

Ripcord grinned. "Maybe I *do* like this plan."

"Maybe not," Duke said.

The grin froze on Rip's face.

"Make out that tree near the corner?" Duke asked. He watched as his friend strained to see. "You're going to shimmy out that branch and drop onto the catwalk. Subdue the guard—"

"Without hurting him, I suppose," Rip interrupted sourly.

Duke nodded. "If possible."

"What do you suggest, the Vulcan nerve pinch?"

"I don't care if it's the Tennessee waltz, just so he's knocked out cold."

"Then what?"

Duke nodded toward the tree. "I'll follow you down the same branch, then join you on the catwalk."

"You follow me to the catwalk, check—then what?"

Duke shrugged. "Then we find Ansalmo."

"Just like that?"

"Just like that," Duke said. "Adding in Stearns taking the place of the guard on the wall, and us encountering dozens of monks with machine guns."

"Let's give my knock-on-the-door plan another look."

Duke just stared at him.

"Or," Rip said, "we could just go climb a tree."

Ten minutes later, at the corner of the monastery, Duke hugged the tree trunk. He was a good twenty feet up, watching as Ripcord shimmied out onto the branch that overhung the catwalk.

In the pitch-dark, even Duke had trouble spotting his friend flattened against the huge branch. The guard, dressed in the plain brown robe and hood of a monk, was heading their way at a slow pace, puffing on a cigarette, AK–47 held loosely in one hand. He'd need the eyes of a night predator to see Ripcord among the foliage.

Yet as the guard got closer to Rip, Duke found his breath coming in shallower gasps as he willed the sentry to not see his friend. As Lopez had told them, these were policemen, not soldiers, and the guard meandered along like a cop walking his beat.

When the guard got to the end of the catwalk, just under Rip, Duke's breathing stopped completely as the guard dawdled, stubbing out a non-monkish cigarette under his foot.

Just when Rip seemed about to reach down and grab the bastard, a loud voice said, *"Informame."*

Duke's Spanish was just good enough to get, "Report in."

"Estación uno, bueno."

"Estación dos, bueno."

And so on they went. From somewhere within his robe, the guard withdrew a walkie-talkie and, at the appropriate moment, said, *"Estación seis, bueno."*

"*Bien*," said the voice in the walkie-talkie, and Duke found himself able to breathe again.

Sticking the walkie-talkie back into the folds of his robe, the guard turned and started back across the catwalk.

The machine gun–carrying monk was maybe three steps into his return trip when Rip dropped silently to the walkway, behind him. The guard took one more step before he realized someone was there. As the monk spun, bringing his weapon up with him, Rip swept the guard's legs and—when the guy thudded onto the walkway—cracked him on the side of the head with the butt of his Glock.

And the guard took an impromptu nap break.

Duke dropped down onto the walkway and Stearns came right behind him. He and Rip waited while Stearns threw on the monk's robe and picked up the religious artifact known as an AK–47. They tied the good brother up with the robe belt, then gagged him with his own sock. Not pretty, but effective.

The stairs to the ground floor were at the far end of the parapet. The pair wasted no time getting over there, Duke looking back to see Stearns patrolling like any other guard in monk drag. Backs against the wall, they silently descended the stairs and came out in one corner of the courtyard.

Crossing was impossible, without getting spotted by the guards at the gate or the back, or by the two rovers. The first door to the left was the chapel, which Duke hoped connected with the monks' dormitory, where he figured to find the vice president.

But first they had to get into the chapel without any of the guards seeing them, and then not run into any *Guardia Nacional* men within.

Using hand signals, Duke told Rip that he'd lead the way with Rip bringing up the rear.

Rip nodded.

The guards at the gate were chatting in Spanish, the two at the back door slumped there, not asleep but not exactly alert. One of the monastery's two rovers was over checking on the granary. The other was thirty feet away and coming toward them.

Duke dissolved into the darkness under the stairs, pressing Rip's arm for him to do the same, which he did. The guard passed and Duke let out his breath. Hurting any of these men would not aid him in gaining Ansalmo's trust, and killing his bodyguards also would hardly win the man over. . . .

Sliding from under the stairs, keeping an eye on the roving guard who moved away from them, Duke slipped to the chapel door—an old wooden slab with no windows. Only way to see what—or who—was within was to open the thing. . . .

So he did.

The chapel was little more than an adobe-walled chamber with a few wooden benches serving as pews before a simple altar. A lone monk knelt there and Duke crept up behind him. As Duke neared the altar, he could feel the air change, and he glanced back to see that Rip had entered, too, and shut the door behind him.

The monk began to rise, and in three quick steps Duke got to him. The monk turned in to Duke's raised Glock, its silencer-adorned snout at the monk's eye level. The man blanched in horror—Duke was standing face-to-face with one of the *real* monks of the monastery. . . .

He and Rip quickly bound the monk and gagged the poor beggar. Then they found a door that led into the first of the two stories of dormitory, via a long hallway.

"You think tying up that monk'll get us time in purgatory," Rip asked, "or just send us straight to hell?"

"Long as we're there in time for breakfast, I don't give a damn."

At the far end of the hall, a guard waited with four more robed gunmen playing poker at the monks' dining table.

Simply no way to get around them.

Duke did not want to double back, to try to find a second-floor access. Time was starting to work against them, leaving only one thing to do, which was plow ahead.

He whispered to Rip, "Try not to kill anybody."

"Haven't all day," Rip pointed out.

Duke stepped out of the hallway. The first guard was so surprised, he just stood there dumbfounded while Duke clocked him upside the head with the pistol. The guy fell like he'd been shot, making a loud *whump*.

As the four poker players looked up in wide-eyed surprise, Rip moved around Duke. One player tried to rise but Rip jumped onto the table and kicked the guy in the face, sending him tumbling over the hard wooden bench, taking his neighbor with him as they fell rudely to the floor. Spinning, Rip kicked one more in the head, dropping him as Duke clipped the fourth one with the pistol, knocking him out cold.

The two on the ground got to their feet growling, but never had a chance—Rip and Duke were on them like stink on skunk, and within seconds the two guards were as unconscious as their brother monks.

The duo took the stairs to the second floor, two at a time, throwing open the doors to the simple cells, quickly dispatching two more guards before they opened the third door to find a monk already rising from his small cot, an automatic pistol in his right hand.

A monk named Jose Ansalmo.

The vice president started to raise the gun, but Duke had the drop on him and raised his own pistol to Ansalmo's eye level.

"Please don't, Mr. President," Duke said.

That took Ansalmo by surprise. "Mr. President?"

"That's what I figure you are, with Vicente gone. We're friendlies. Lower the gun and let's talk."

The man's eyes were tight with distrust. "You are here to *kill* me. Why should there be talk?"

"If we were here to kill you, there wouldn't be. We're a U.S. Army insertion team sent to help you."

Relief washed Ansalmo's lean, intelligent face. "So then, the traitor Lopez is under arrest, and peace has been restored?"

"Not quite that simple, sir."

Ansalmo frowned in confusion.

"We were also sent here by General Lopez to kill you."

The man's eyebrows hiked. "Then perhaps I should *keep* the gun. . . ."

"This is a covert operation, Mr. President, and we are posing as mercenaries. We fooled Lopez into hiring us to come in and kill you, when our real mission is to free you. Clear enough?"

From behind Duke, Rip said, "It better be—there's going to be more guards coming any second now."

"Mr. President," Duke said, "we know you're the rightful leader of your country . . . but the U.S. cannot simply march in openly and make everything all right."

Ansalmo nodded. "The Middle East proved as much."

That stopped Duke for just a moment. Then: "Which is why we're here covertly, sir. It was the only way to find out where you were. Now, we have to get you out of here, before Lopez and his *federales* come around to kill all of us."

Ansalmo was putting the pieces together. He touched a forefinger to the air, as if writing there. "Lopez uses you to kill me, then kills *you* . . . and claims you're working for the rebels."

"Or, because we're Americans, he blames the U.S.A."

With a nod, Ansalmo said, "Either way, he gets his wish—my death, and his virtual coronation. With his filthy hands looking clean."

"That's the game, sir."

"The *puta*'s son is even smarter than I thought—more ruthless too." Ansalmo's eyes narrowed shrewdly and traveled from Duke to Rip and back again. "But why should I believe that *this* isn't a trap? Part of an even more clever scheme? You could be here to lure me out of the monastery to kill me."

Duke said, "Sir, if I wanted you dead, you would have long since been dead—my partner and I would already be over the wall and on our way back to San Marco . . . if we were fool enough to trust General Lopez, that is. When we leave here, you'll see that we have not seriously harmed any of your men. Some may be unconscious for a while, but we could have killed all of them . . . and we didn't. Call that a show of good faith."

Ansalmo asked, "Then why didn't you just come to the gate and ask for me?"

Duke could sense Rip, behind him, giving him a look. "Because not only were we sent here to kill you, we have to assume that Lopez has someone watching, to make sure we carry out the plan, as advertised."

"So . . . you have to give them a show."

Duke half smiled. "We do have to make it look like we're trying, yes, sir."

The vice president's eyes spelled it out: He believed them now.

Ansalmo said, "Tell me your name, soldier."

"You can call me Duke, sir. That's enough."

"All right, Duke—I'm in your hands. What do we do next?"

Rip said, "Better come up with a plan *fast*—more guards in bathrobes are headed our way."

Footsteps pounded on the stairs and in the corridor outside.

Knowing there was only one thing to do, Duke spun his pistol and handed it butt first to President Ansalmo.

Ansalmo accepted the gift with a nod.

Guards in monk's robes, automatic weapons leveled at Rip and Duke, poured into the room. Thankfully, the cell was only large enough to hold three or four of them, but with their guns pointed at Duke and Rip, that seemed more than sufficient.

A voice in the hallway said, "Let me through—let me *through*!"

A pair of guards backed out to make room for the man. Like Ansalmo and the rest, he wore a monk's robe. He was of medium height, but his bearing made him seem taller. His face was a mask of anger, dark eyes burning into Duke.

"How the hell did you get in here?" he demanded.

Rip, his hands in the air, said "Language, padre, language. . . ."

Duke, hands up, took another step toward him. "Take it easy."

"I *said*—"

Ansalmo stepped between the men. "Roberto, *calmate*. They are our friends—part of a rescue team from the United States."

The man was shaking his head. "And how do you know this? How can you be *sure* this is not more of Lopez's treachery?"

Holding up the pistol Duke had given him, Ansalmo said, "He just handed me his weapon. They are *friends,* Roberto, here to help us."

"You're Roberto Romero," Duke asked. "head of the *Guardia Nacional*?"

Romero's black hair was thick, his eyes a deep brown in a pockmarked, mustached face. Though his anger appeared to have dissipated, his mistrust had not.

"You've done your homework," he said to Duke. "You know me, but I do not know you."

"You can call me Duke."

With an almost imperceptible nod toward Rip, Romero said, "I assume your friend has no surname either."

"It's a Madonna or Shakira type thing," Rip said. "And call me Ripcord."

"And why," an unimpressed Romero asked, "are we expected to trust you?"

"Trust us," Duke said, keeping emotion out of his voice, "only if you want to live."

"If that's a *threat*—"

Ansalmo said, "Roberto, General Lopez is on his way here, right now—to double-cross our friends, and murder us. We must *leave.* We must go with these men, and we must go *now.*"

Still not quite with the program, Romero asked, "Where will we go?"

"That," Duke said to the vice president, "is an excellent question."

Ansalmo's expression grew thoughtful. Then he asked, "Might I make a suggestion?"

CHAPTER EIGHT
Rebel Rouser

San Sebastiao

Scarlett O'Hara was ready, even eager for action. She roosted next to a tree, her red ponytail tucked into the collar of her camouflage fatigues, her gas-propulsion crossbow pistol poised, as she kept her eyes trained on two members of the American team in the near darkness. She and her unit had been shadowing the American insertion team all night, and she was growing weary of watching.

The lovely redhead was not accustomed to playing babysitter, which was what this backup support assignment amounted to. She was devoted to her duty, and would take on a tank single-handedly or type up reports at a desk without complaint.

But all this wait-and-watch was not her preference—she told herself that it was an inefficient, even illogical waste of her highly honed skills, and those of the rest of Unit Alpha, to be subjected to this secondary status. Truth be told, she simply liked being in the thick of it, but a scientifically minded type like Scarlett could never admit to anyone (including herself) that the rush of battle was her raison d'être.

Snake Eyes was once again tagging along anonymously atop one of Lopez's tanks, sending messages about the general's progress toward the monastery. They were still a ways out but coming up fast. Maybe Scarlett wouldn't have to wait long for action, after all. . . .

The JOE unit knew the location of every member of the insertion team and would stay out of their way; but they were also prepared to intervene against Lopez's forces, if need be. The focus of the JOE team's mission remained the pulse weapons. Snake Eyes had watched the loading of the trucks, tanks, and even Lopez's personal Humvee, and had reported no sighting of the elusive next-gen weapons.

Maybe Gung Ho's theory was on-target: that Lopez had the weapons, but wouldn't use them again until he was cleared of President Vicente's assassination. The general was coming up behind his "mercenary" team with troops and firepower, but seemingly *without* the pulse weapons. . . .

The Americans were now scattered around the perimeter of the monastery—they, too, appeared to realize Lopez was on the way—and the JOE team was scattered, as well.

Snake Eyes was with Lopez's convoy, while Scarlett was out back, in the jungle, eyes on the sniper and the M–60 machine-gun position. Heavy Duty was one hundred yards up from the monastery, his machine gun trained on the road, just in case. Breaker and Gung Ho were on either side of the monastery, monitoring the Americans.

Scarlett's wrist communicator vibrated—a message from Snake Eyes: FIVE KLICKS OUT.

Two Americans, Hauser and Weems, had been inside the monastery for a good while. She wondered what the hell was going on in there. If the American team didn't haul tail out soon, both Able Team and Unit Alpha would be in the middle•of a major firefight. Scarlett may have craved action, but that didn't extend to playing sitting duck when Lopez showed up with a couple dozen men and his tanks. . . .

Gung Ho's voice in her earpiece said: *"We have movement in the monastery."*

She turned and gazed down into the courtyard. Nice thing about being up here, watching, was that she could make out most of the courtyard activity. She saw a truck back out of the barn, followed by a car—someone moving out.

But who?

Earlier, Gung Ho had speculated that the Americans had found the missing vice president, Ansalmo. And the notion was a good one—the Americans hadn't exactly gone to that monastery for religious guidance. That they were seeking Ansalmo made sense.

Made sense that Ansalmo would have hidden out in the fortresslike monastery. Made sense that the Americans might sell General Lopez a bill of goods that they were mercenaries and could storm the citadel and kidnap the vice president. And made perfect sense Lopez would betray his mercenaries to assassinate Ansalmo, with a bunch of Americans or maybe rebels to blame for it.

As Scarlett watched, monks with automatic weapons came out into the yard and looked around for threats, as they took up posts near the vehicles.

Interesting vows they must have taken, she thought. *Any vow of silence apparently wouldn't include gunfire. . . .*

Around her, Scarlett felt the sniper and machine-gun nest getting ready to move. She pressed herself deeper into the darkness. A man with an M–60 headed down the hill, the sniper coming behind him, passing within five feet of Scarlett and having no idea she was there.

She watched the Americans go down the hill, giving them time to get to the rear of the monastery. When that door opened, she reported in: "They're bugging out."

"Roger that," Gung Ho said. *"Form up on Heavy Duty. Lopez will be along any minute."*

"Roger," Scarlett said.

Breaker rogered the transmission as well.

Everybody was moving at once down there; but the question nagging Scarlett was . . . where the hell were they *going?*

The monks and most of Able Team got themselves loaded into the truck. Duke and Rip joined Ansalmo and Romero in a black Mercedes sedan equipped with bulletproof glass. Security guru Romero sat up front with the driver while Ripcord and Duke settled in on either side of Ansalmo.

The Mercedes took the lead, following directions Ansalmo had provided. Their plan took them in the opposite direction from their pursuers. That kept Lopez and his men behind them, but not following them, at least not yet, because the San Sebastiaoan contingent would first stop at the monastery, to make a delivery of wholesale slaughter.

The flaw would be this: Everyone Lopez was after was gone, Ansalmo and Romero and the mercenaries, too, the real monks having headed for the hills, at Ansalmo's insistence.

"You really think this will work?" Duke asked the new president, as their short convoy took a right onto a four-lane highway and sped west into the night.

Ansalmo, crammed between Duke and Rip, managed to shrug, despite the tight space. "It should be the last thing Lopez would expect."

"Got *that* right," Rip said.

Ansalmo gave Rip a curious look.

"No offense intended, Mr. President, it's just that it's the last thing *we* thought you'd do, too. So it ought to throw Lopez for a loop."

Ansalmo nodded gravely. "My friends . . . we have been fighting this rebellion for too long. I tried to convince President Vicente to take this course, but he could not bring himself to. He did not feel he was in a position to risk such a thing. *We* are."

"Making a deal with the rebels," Duke said. He smiled wryly and shook his head. "I can see why Vicente would have had qualms."

"Qualms perhaps, Duke, but he was not against it, not in principle. Like myself, Martin Vicente felt he'd been elected to serve the greater good of *all* the citizens of San Sebastiao."

From the front seat came a cold response from Romero, who'd gone on record against the plan the president had conceived, and which they were now carrying out.

"The rebels," Romero said, "forfeited their citizenship when they turned against the rightfully elected government."

Without rancor, Ansalmo said, "I would expect such a remark from the likes of Lopez, Roberto—not you."

Romero turned, his face revealing the pain that remark had caused. "But how can you compromise with traitors?"

"To govern, you have to be willing to compromise. And from the point of view of the rebels, they are patriots, and we are the traitors."

"You call them patriots," Romero said. "I call them wild animals. And you cannot compromise with wild animals."

"They are men, my friend. Men who have hopes and dreams for this country, too. . . . Perhaps, we can minimize our differences and combine our common goals to make this country as great as it could be."

"Assuming," Duke said, "we can *find* the rebels."

"My concern," Romero said, "is that they may find us first . . . and will not have the idealistic humanitarian bent of my esteemed brother-in-law."

Duke asked, "Are there rebels in this area?"

"They are everywhere," Romero said. "Sometimes

in small numbers, sometimes in force. However, the man we're seeking—"

"So," Duke cut in, "we don't know where we're going?"

Ansalmo said, "We have a general idea. The man we need to talk to is Benito Rojas—the leader of the rebellion."

"He calls himself *General* Rojas," Romero said, a nasty edge in his voice.

Duke asked, "Is he a former military man who once held that rank?"

"To be honest," Ansalmo said, " 'General' is what others call him. He wears no uniform and I have never heard of him referring to himself in that way."

Romero chuckled. "He's a *campesino*—a farmer."

"A very *smart* farmer," Ansalmo added. "Rojas was one of many voices speaking out, saying that the oil bubbling beneath our soil should belong to San Sebastiao—that the money generated by the black riches should be spread among all the people, and not allowed to make foreigners wealthy."

Duke asked, "Are you in disagreement?"

"His approach is radical and extreme, though his sentiments I share. I believe there are many ways for the people of our country to prosper. Our administration has one plan, the rebels have another, less-*patient* plan."

Rip said, "I bet Lopez has a plan, too, and I kinda think 'patient' wouldn't cover it."

Duke said to the president, "But despite common concerns, you and Rojas are enemies?"

Ansalmo nodded.

"Okay," Duke said. "Answer me this. Would he kill you before you two had the chance to talk?"

Ansalmo forced another cramped little shrug. "I would hope not."

Rip said, "Man, *that's* reassuring. . . ."

Ansalmo continued: "Rojas and I have never met. I know that he is nonviolent, a reactive warrior, a rebel who destroys property, not people. Of course, there are those who commit violence in his name . . . whether with or without his blessing. That is something about which we are uncertain."

"So you're sayin'," Rip said, "even if we find this dude, he might try to kill us all."

But it was Duke who answered: "Staying at the monastery wasn't an option. Waiting for the general and half the soldiers in San Sebastiao wasn't, either. You got any other ideas?"

Rip shook his head. "Just that we gotta get off this highway before the sun comes up."

"No argument there," Duke said. He tapped Romero on the shoulder and the man glanced back. "Aren't all government vehicles equipped with GPS?"

This earned a small smile from Romero. "They *were*. But when President Ansalmo began to worry about General Lopez's ambitions, this car and the truck behind us conveniently developed problems with their GPS units."

Rip asked, "What kind of 'problems'?"

"They were removed and never replaced."

"Good thinking," Duke said. "We'll still need to ditch all of these wheels, though—too easy to spot from the air, after daybreak. Is there somewhere we could change vehicles? Somewhere Lopez wouldn't consider immediately?"

"*Sí,*" Romero said, without a beat. "Ciudad Pacífica."

"Where's that?"

"Another twenty kilometers or so."

"Got a map?"

Romero took a map from the glove compartment and handed it back. Duke unfolded it and Rip provided a mini-flashlight beam, asking the president, "Where's this Ciudad Pacífica?"

Ansalmo pointed it out.

Duke folded the map and passed it forward. "Let's find a route that gets us off this highway," he said. "You're *sure* this place is safe from Lopez?"

"Should be the safest place for us," Romero said. "The home city of Benito Rojas—he is beloved there, while Lopez and the military are despised. Lopez's men have regularly come to Ciudad Pacífica, looking for him, and the general's methods are brutal—houses burned, people beaten. The citizens of Ciudad Pacífica will not inform on us to Lopez—they hate the military far more than they ever hated either Jose or President Vicente."

Rip grinned. "That makes Ciudad Pacífica my favorite new vacation spot."

Ansalmo asked Duke, "Do you have a cellphone?"

"Sure, why?"

"I need to make a call, and we wouldn't want General Lopez to get a GPS fix on *my* phone. I'm assuming he can't trace yours."

The guy was no fool—Duke handed the president his cell. "Who are you calling, sir?"

For a moment, Ansalmo said nothing, just looked at the glowing face of the cellphone in the dark. Then he said, "There is a certain man—a member of Rojas's inner circle. A real patriot."

Rip smirked. "And a real double agent?"

"No," Ansalmo insisted. "He is loyal to Rojas, but . . . he owes a debt to me."

Rip asked, "Money kinda debt?"

"Something more important than money," Ansalmo said. "Honor."

The call, entirely in Spanish, lasted perhaps seven minutes. Though he could read and speak a number of languages, Duke's Spanish was only rudimentary, and hearing only one side of the conversation meant he came away with precious little. Further, Ansalmo's expression revealed nothing as he spoke.

When he hung up, Ansalmo smiled. "The man has paid his debt in full."

Duke asked, "He told you where Rojas is?"

"*Sí.* General Lopez's troops visited Ciudad Pacífica immediately following Vicente's assassination. Evidently, Lopez hoped to remove Rojas as well. Killing Vicente, Rojas, and myself? That would have given the general a clear path toward assuming complete control."

"That it would," Duke said. Not exactly a chess move, but the general knew his checkers.

"After Lopez left," Ansalmo continued, "Rojas returned to the city . . . and my contact says he is still there."

"That's a break," Duke said. "Any way for us to

contact Rojas, without just waltzing in and maybe getting shot?"

Ansalmo said, "Perhaps—Rojas is a devout Catholic. Every day, just after breakfast, he goes to church to pray."

"How many churches in Ciudad Pacífica?"

Holding up his index finger, Ansalmo said, "It is not a very big town."

"Good," Duke said, with a curt nod. "Then we're set."

Rip blinked. "Are we?"

"Sure," Duke said, and his eyes met Ansalmo's. "General Rojas is going to church, and we're going to have a monk ready, to hear his confession."

Anger boiled within General Pedro Lopez as he stood outside the main gate at the monastery of the Brotherhood of the Servants of Santa Maria.

"*Abandoned?*" he roared.

"*Sí,* abandoned, *mi general,*" Lieutenant Hernandez was timidly saying. "There is no one within these walls. We have seen not even a scurrying mouse."

"*Coño!* They could not *disappear*!"

"It is as if they have, *mi general.* There is fresh food and drink in the hampers. There is—"

"I do not want an inventory of *things*! Find the people! Find them *now*!"

"*Inmediatamente, mi general!*"

As Hernandez dashed off, Lopez called behind him: "Send up the helicopters. These pigs have to be *somewhere*! *Find* them!"

Hernandez climbed quickly into the general's Humvee and got on the radio.

Stomping through the gate and into the courtyard, Lopez seethed as he realized that he had been swindled. Obviously, the mercenaries had not killed Ansalmo, apparently kidnapping him for their own purposes. This much was evident.

But so many other questions swirled in his mind. Why would the mercenaries have spared the monks and Ansalmo's guards? The Americans did not have the vehicles, much less any reason to take so many living bodies along for what would be a dangerous journey . . . whatever that journey might be. But why drive them out and away from the monastery?

Could the Americans have been smart enough to anticipate the massacre that Lopez would have brought down upon the monks and their guests?

Had the mercenaries taken Ansalmo hostage, thinking they could raise the ante for his death? Worse yet, were they now somehow in league with the vice president? If so, why? *How?* Had Ansalmo made them a better offer? How was that even possible? Trapped in this monastery, Ansalmo had nothing to offer . . . did he?

So many questions, so few answers. And the hardest of them: *How to proceed?*

Usually even the most complicated problems could be reduced to simplicity by the ruthless San Sebastiaoan general. He assumed that everyone who did not agree with him was an enemy, and all enemies were out to destroy him, and all enemies should be exterminated. Expect the worst and prepare for it—anything less would be a pleasant surprise.

That was exactly how he would approach this new setback—expecting the worst. Lopez had enemies—Ansalmo and his cronies, the rebels, and now, the team of Americans. . . .

Assuming that Ansalmo and the mercenaries had joined forces, what would their next move be? They would of course avoid Lopez, although they did not necessarily know how close the general and his forces were.

Ansalmo needed help to survive, much less prevail.

The man had stayed penned up in the monastery because he did not have the army behind him. The mercenaries were good, but they could not single-handedly defeat Lopez's troops; so they would need help. Where might they find it?

And suddenly the general knew: *Ansalmo and the mercenaries would combine forces with the rebels.*

Still, Lopez knew little about the actual destination of his enemies. If Ansalmo was going to join the rebels, that meant he would have to track Rojas down. And if Lopez could have tracked Rojas down, he would have done so and killed the *bastardo* long ago.

If Ansalmo and the mercenaries had headed back to San Marco, their convoy would have met the general's on the road. Obviously, they were headed in the opposite direction . . . but toward what destination? The vice president couldn't stay on the road long, without being spotted.

No, Ansalmo would be heading somewhere relatively close—he would *have* to, especially with the mercenaries and his bodyguards along for the ride—at least twenty men, if not more. Hiding would be hard for so large a group.

Hernandez returned, anxiety coming off the man like heat off hot asphalt. "*Mi general,* the helicopters are flying, but they will not see much until first light."

Nodding his disappointment, Lopez said, "Get the men back into the truck."

"Yes, sir."

As Hernandez turned to carry out the order, Lopez asked, "Where does our most recent intelligence place Rojas?"

The apprehensive Hernandez glanced back. "Nowhere, I'm afraid. We have lost him. No one has reported seeing him for weeks. There have been no rebel communications that we have been able to track. The man is a ghost."

His anger subsided, Lopez bestowed on his lieutenant a ghastly smile. "Then let us start by checking out our ghost's old haunts. Ciudad Pacífica, down the road, is not far. We will start our search there."

At his post in the nearby jungle, Gung Ho smiled to himself—he'd been enjoying General Lopez's temper tantrum, though the man had cooled now, and was climbing into his Humvee, ready to head out.

Things were looking up.

Snake Eyes had dismounted from the tank he'd

been riding when the general's convoy had approached the monastery, and had managed to find a new position, up a tree, close enough to hear every word of the general's conversation with his subordinate. He had then conveyed the general's destination to Gung Ho.

When Lopez and his convoy moved out, the JOE team broke from its hiding places and piled into the 1986 Toyota Cressida that served as its transportation on this trip. Procured back in San Marco from a neighborhood near where Joaquin and Antonia lived, the car—like many in San Sebastiao—wasn't much to look at, but ran well enough. Anyway, it was faster than Lopez's convoy, especially the tanks.

Though they would have to take an alternate route, Gung Ho did know (thanks to Snake Eyes) where they all were going. Even as he pulled the vehicle onto the road, Breaker was communicating with the Pit, getting alternate directions to Ciudad Pacífica.

Gung Ho drove and Scarlett rode shotgun, while Snake Eyes and Heavy Duty bracketed Breaker in the backseat.

"Real high-tech transport," Heavy D grumbled.

"Beats walkin'," Gung Ho pointed out.

"The next left," Breaker said from the backseat. Smaller than the others, the trimly bearded communications expert had an eyepiece that served as a remote computer station, and could access more information than your average mainframe. "There's a two-lane road that takes us to another two-lane road, and so on and so on."

Gung Ho asked, "How far out of the way are we going?"

"Ten or fifteen klicks."

Gung Ho sped up, turning left onto the two-lane road. "Find out everything you can about this Ciudad Whatever."

"Already on it," Breaker said.

"And try to get a fix on where Ansalmo is going, and why."

"On it," Breaker said.

"Good," Gung Ho said. " 'Cause I want to know where we're going, when we're gonna be there, where we're setting up, and what the hell is going to be going down in front of us."

"I," Breaker said smoothly, "am on it."

The truck and the Mercedes were once again hidden away, the car in a barn on a farm about five klicks outside town, the truck in the jungle nearby. Able Team—along with Ansalmo, Romero, and the *Guardia Nacional* men—had trooped in on foot.

Duke had been favorably impressed by the new president of San Sebastiao. Though wearing a monk's robe and sandals, Ansalmo had marched the five klicks into Ciudad Pacífica without complaint. They made it to the edge of town easily, the team and Romero's men setting up a flimsy perimeter around the small town.

Bergman and his M–60 were facing the main road. Peters, the sniper, was on the side of town where they'd walked in. If Lopez found the vehicles, and came in from the farm, the sniper would pick them off. Alternating with Romero's men, the balance of Able Team was set up in and around the town.

Ciudad Pacífica's five hundred souls were packed into one square mile of buildings, split almost evenly between brick and adobe—a sleepy little bump in the road, with a bank, a restaurant, a few bars, a gas station, and a small *groceria*. The two most prominent buildings were the city hall and, across the town square, the church. If Norman Rockwell had picked a South American hamlet for a *Saturday Evening Post* cover, Ciudad Pacífica would have done nicely.

Only four from their party had come into town. Duke, Rip, Ansalmo, and Romero—now all wearing monk's robes—had wound their way to the square.

The sun was up now, and they were in the church. The only priest—middle-aged, balding Father Tomas—seemed at first stunned to see the live Ansalmo before him; then he became respectfully suspicious. . . .

"Señor *Vice Presidente,* may I inquire what brings you to our humble church? And . . . dressed as a brother?"

Ansalmo smiled gently and said, "I am sorry if you are offended, Father, but cloaking ourselves in these robes was a necessary evil, for the safety of myself and these men."

"I see." The padre's smile was also a gentle one. "Disguising oneself from those who would do harm is no evil, my son."

"Thank you, Father. As for why I'm here. . . ."

Ansalmo explained the situation.

He concluded by saying: "I give you my word as a servant of the people and a good Catholic son . . . what I tell you is true."

The priest clapped his hands together. "This is what we have been *praying* for—a bringing together of the people as one Christian nation."

"I appreciate your prayers, Father . . . but right now I need more corporeal assistance. . . ."

Fifteen minutes later, Romero stood watch in the church's bell tower, while Rip, outside, guarded the entrance from a nearby hiding spot. Inside, Duke positioned himself in a short hallway behind the confessional, near the priest's side (where Ansalmo already sat). From here, Duke could see both the front entry and a door down the hall, behind which a storage room provided a possible entry point, with only a flimsy window as a barrier.

In his earpiece, Rip's voice announced, *"Three headed your way."*

"Roger that," Duke whispered.

A second later, Rip said, *"Two coming in, one hanging by the door."*

Duke melted into the shadows when the church's big wooden door swung out and two men strode in, one a strapping guy in jeans and a T-shirt, his curly black hair short, the other heavier but shorter and less muscular, more an accountant type than the leader of a rebellion.

Pushing fifty, with wispy black hair, thick glasses, and a grave demeanor, Benito Rojas wore no Castro-esque fatigues nor any garish, al-Gadhafi-type uniform, but rather jeans, cowboy boots, and a white dress shirt buttoned to the collar.

Just inside, the pair dipped fingers into a simple bowl of holy water and made the sign of the cross. Duke watched as the two walked to the rear of the pews and genuflected. A bulge in the back of the bodyguard's T-shirt told Duke that the man had not come to the church unarmed.

The bodyguard hung back as Rojas moved to the front of the church, the leader locking eyes with the looming ceramic Jesus on the cross above the altar, until he paused to genuflect again.

Rojas stopped before a wrought-iron tiered stand of candles, some lighted, some not. The rebel leader stood mute, praying, then lit a candle, returned to the altar, genuflected again, and came back down the aisle, rejoining his bodyguard. They passed Duke, who for a moment thought the rebel was about to exit without making confession.

Then Rojas turned toward the confessional. Duke rapped lightly on the wooden panel, alerting the man within, after which Duke disappeared deeper into the hallway.

In the confessional, Jose Ansalmo sat with his thoughts and the sounds of his own ragged breathing. He wasn't really afraid so much as he was anticipating this chance to save his country from the military despotism of Pedro Lopez. Sweat conspired to make the wool monk's robe even itchier and rougher. The tight space held heat like an oven but Ansalmo knew he was flushed with anxiety as much as temperature.

When the almost imperceptible knock came, Ansalmo all but jumped. Then followed the small rustle of a worshiper settling beyond the screen.

"Bless me, Father, for I have sinned," said the quiet voice. "It has been twenty-four hours since my last—"

Ansalmo interrupted the rebel leader by sliding back the screen and framing himself in the window where, even in the dim light, Rojas could clearly see him.

"*You,*" Rojas said, his shock almost comically obvious. Then the rebel leader reached for the door handle and rose to his feet.

"Benito, please do not go," Ansalmo said. "We need to talk. I have, in part, sought you out in this holy place because it represents sanctuary for us both."

Rojas sat back down, his eyes still wide, not with shock now, but rather skepticism.

"I beseech you to speak with me," Ansalmo said, "for the sake of our beloved country's safety."

"You are not here to secure my arrest?" Rojas asked tentatively.

"No," Ansalmo said. "I do not agree with the methods of the rebellion, but I share your desire for change, and to make things better for all the people of our country."

Rojas said nothing, but he was listening. He *was* listening. . . .

"You think I represent a threat to you and your ideals," Ansalmo said.

"That is because you do," Rojas said.

"And I feel the same way about the rebels."

The remark was greeted by silence.

Ansalmo said, "Yet we both know there is a greater danger to San Sebastiao than either the rebels or the administration."

"Lopez," Rojas said.

"Lopez," Ansalmo agreed.

"And that is why you are here?"

"Yes. To battle this evil man, we must seek to find a way to overcome our differences."

"How can I trust you?" Rojas asked. "For all I know, you had Vicente killed yourself, in order to assume his chair."

"Good God, man," Ansalmo said, forgetting where he was. "He was my best friend, my most trusted ally—I tried to *save* him!"

"The question stands," Rojas said firmly. "How can I trust you?"

"The same way I am trusting you—by choosing to. Don't you think I know you could have your men kill me, before I even leave this confessional? I choose to trust you, as a man of honor and hope. Choose to trust *me* on those same grounds . . . because there is more at stake than you and me. This is for our country. We must work together."

After a moment's thought, Rojas said, "I am willing to consider setting terms for negotiations."

Ansalmo's laugh was quiet yet bitter. "You do not understand, Benito. We must come to an accord now. *Here*. You see, Lopez is on his way to kill us *both*."

Rojas's face furrowed. "And how do you know this?"

"Americans the general hired to kill me have instead helped me. They know Lopez's plan. I believe them."

The rebel's eyes had a wildness now. "But it could be a trap set by Lopez, to get us together and kill us both!"

Ansalmo shrugged and said, "We are both still alive, are we not? Two of the Americans are with me now."

Rojas frowned. "Here in Ciudad Pacífica?"

"Right here in this church," Ansalmo said. "If they were going to kill us, we would both have been dead by now."

Rojas considered this for a long moment. "What do you propose?"

"That we join forces to defeat Lopez."

"And then?"

"Within six months, new democratic elections."

"*Three* months."

"Three months then," Ansalmo assented. "I will run for president, and I would like you to run as my vice president."

Now it was Rojas's turn to laugh. "What makes you think that I won't run against you?"

"I would expect you to, Benito. But I would urge you to join me instead, because we both know that outside forces are trying to influence what happens within San Sebastiao."

"You mean this scoundrel Chernitz," Rojas said.

"He is but the first. You have spoken with him?"

"Yes," Rojas admitted.

"Then you know the kind of death he is peddling. These new weapons of his are the kind that open wounds that do not heal over decades. Separately, you and I are formidable men—either could lead this country, and I believe lead it well. But as a *team* we would be even stronger. This country, our home, could become the paradise on this earth that God intended her to be."

Rojas seemed to be absorbing these words.

"Time is running out," Ansalmo said. "Lopez will be here soon, and the die will be cast."

"I have one question," Rojas said.

"Yes?"

"Who *are* these Americans?"

"They are a combat team sent by the U.S. to help me keep the country from coming apart. A clandestine operation. Covert."

"How many?"

"Ten men."

"Ten?" Rojas asked. "What can ten men do?"

"I have seen them do much today. But in any case, with the help of my *Guardia Nacional* detail and *your* men, perhaps we can prevail."

"I have very few men," Rojas said with a sigh and a headshake. "Most of those who claim to be with the rebellion act independently. Those who commit violence against our own people—they have nothing to do with us."

"How many do you have here?"

"Today? Six."

For several long moments, Ansalmo contemplated that.

Rojas asked, "How many men do *you* have?"

"Twenty from the Guardia Nacional and the ten Americans."

"And how many does Lopez bring?"

"I have no numbers. But we must remember, he is head of the military for the whole country."

Rojas laughed out loud.

"Does this amuse you?" Ansalmo asked coldly.

"I apologize for my laughter. But this is so absurd—thirty-eight against an army."

"You're probably right, but I am afraid I do not see the humor."

"I was laughing," the rebel said, "because I have decided to accept your proposal."

Ansalmo nodded, a priest passing benediction.

Rojas went on: "We will join forces now, and—if we are fortunate enough to survive General Lopez's best efforts—we will run together for office . . . although we may wish to negotiate, at a future date, which of us heads the ticket."

Ansalmo smiled. "Fair enough, my friend."

"But you must admit the absurdity—it just seems foolish to discuss the good the two of us might try to achieve, when first we must survive the wrath of Lopez . . . if he is indeed coming."

"Oh, he's coming," Ansalmo said, "and he brings hell with him."

Rojas shrugged and smiled. "Then perhaps it is a good thing we are on hallowed ground."

There was a knock at the door.

"*Sí?*" Ansalmo said.

Duke said, "The general's getting close, Mr. President. We have to go."

"*Sí,*" Ansalmo said. "*Un momento.*" He extended his hand through the small window. "Shall we try to save our country?"

Shaking Ansalmo's hand, Rojas said, "*Sí.*" Then

he shrugged and smiled. "It may be that God is still on our side."

"Does God choose sides in matters of state?"

"He does in matters of good and evil," Rojas said. "In Samuel, when confronting Goliath, David said, 'This is the day the Lord will deliver you into my hand, and I will strike you down, and cut off your head . . . ' "

Ansalmo picked up, " ' . . . that all the earth may know that there is a God in Israel, and that all this assembly may know that Yahweh saves not with sword and spear; for the battle is Yahweh's, and he will give you into our hand.' "

"Yes," Rojas said. "Let us pray that God is not only in Israel, but in San Sebastiao as well."

CHAPTER NINE

JOE in the Game

The Pit

General Hawk was not happy.

In the Control Room, he stood before a massive screen on which Gung Ho's somewhat grainy countenance looked stoically back.

The general said, "And you haven't retrieved the pulse weapons?"

"Not yet, sir."

"How close have you come?"

"Not very."

"Define."

Gung Ho's smile was the sick kind a kid gave his old man, inquiring about the status of homework. "Sir, we haven't *seen* the damn things."

The general twitched back the sicker kind of smile a father gives a child whose homework-status report was unsatisfying. "What *have* you learned?"

"We're just outside a small town, glorified village really—Ciudad Pacífica. Vice President Ansalmo is in the Catholic church there meeting with—"

"Rojas, the rebel leader," Hawk cut in.

"Well, yes, sir."

"I gathered that much from Breaker's earlier background inquiries. What about the American team?"

"Their leader is one cool character, sir. He entered that monastery, manned as it was with twenty men, and waltzed Ansalmo out without firing a shot."

"Noted," Hawk said. "What else?"

"Just the Ansalmo/Rojas meeting. Do you want us to intercede?"

"No," Hawk snapped. "We don't install governments—we support peace. Any decision Ansalmo and Rojas make is their own concern. The pulse weapons are yours. Do you have any notion where they might be?"

Gung Ho swallowed. "Just that that gunrunner Chernitz is still with Lopez. Presumably the weapons have to be with them, somewhere, or in some way easily within their reach."

"I see. Enjoying your tropical vacation?"

"Uh . . . sir, it's no vacation."

"Exactly right. Find the goddamn things!"

And Hawk terminated the video link.

Cover Girl stepped from the darkness. "Is everything all right, sir?"

He managed a smile. "I believe it is. Unit Alpha just needed a little jump start. . . . I'd like to see the record of the American leading Able Team. What's his name again?"

"Hauser, sir. Conrad Hauser—nickname Duke."

Hawk's eyes narrowed. "Right. Same team leader as the Uzekurkistan mission."

"Yes, sir. You want that record electronically?"

"No. Tolerate my Luddite streak, would you, Cover Girl, and bring me a hard-copy file? To my office?"

"No problem, sir."

In his stateroom, sitting at his desk surrounded by framed photos of military service over a long career, Hawk thought about those pulse weapons, and what they might portend for the future of conventional warfare.

Only a matter of time before the damn things were everywhere, he knew . . . but for now, he would do everything he could to keep them off the market.

G.I. JOE already had similar weapons in their own armament inventory, but he had avoided their use in the field, as yet. But if the bad guys got their upgrade, Hawk would have to see that his people got their deadly upgrade, as well.

For now, however, he meant to keep these advanced killing machines out of the hands of evil-doers, though if Lopez used them again, the technological cat would be out of the warfare bag, and proliferation would be impossible to stop.

Hawk had done all he could from the Pit. Gung Ho was an exceptional team leader and had a top unit with him.

And now it was up to them.

San Sebastiao

In the jungle encampment, Breaker approached Gung Ho, who could clearly read his communications officer's tension.

"What?" Gung Ho asked.

"Lopez," Breaker said, twitching a frown. "The general's not moving all the way into the city. His troops are coming in on foot."

"What about the American perimeter?"

Breaker shook his head, and his tone was grim. "Pretty thin. But what's worse is, I intercepted a transmission from Lopez."

"Yeah?"

"He's called in reinforcements and helicopters."

"What do the Americans have to meet that with?"

"Hard to say. There's maybe twenty-five or thirty between the American team and Ansalmo's men. No telling how many rebels—or rebel sympathizers, ready to take up arms—there are in that little town. But unless it's every able-bodied man and woman, I'd say Lopez outnumbers them."

Gung Ho nodded his thanks, then went over to where the team lounged against the scruffy car, waiting for instructions.

"Snake Eyes," Gung Ho said.

The silent assassin straightened.

"We need to make sure Lopez doesn't surprise anybody. Can you make that happen, without giving us away?"

Snake Eyes nodded once, but that was plenty for Gung Ho's peace of mind.

"Good," he said. "Heavy D and I'll get in behind Lopez, and disrupt his flank, and the reinforcements, when they show."

Scarlett was frowning. "Where do I come in?"

"See if you can do something about those choppers."

The lovely redhead smirked. "Sounds like one of those dirty jobs somebody's got to do."

"Somebody being you."

She shrugged. "Beats boredom. Can I get some help from Breaker?"

Gung Ho shook his head. "He's got to watch the car and deal with communications."

"Right," she said. "He can't be bothered with something as trivial as shooting down helicopters."

"Something like that."

"Fine," she said with another shrug. "I've got it covered."

Gung Ho put his fist into the middle of their huddle. The other hands piled on top of his.

"Yo, JOEs!" they all said. Then Gung Ho added, "Let's go!"

And they went.

What had begun as a very bad night for General Pedro Lopez was turning into a very good morning.

Even without GPS, he and his men had found the farm where Ansalmo had stopped, the car he'd arrived in, and finally the truck that had transported his men.

Ansalmo would have come to Ciudad Pacífica for only one reason—to meet with Rojas. And if Rojas was indeed visiting his home village, then Lopez would have them *both*. . . .

Lieutenant Hernandez trotted up to him, the pair standing in the jungle near Ansalmo's abandoned truck.

"Sir, we have scouted the enemy positions."

"And?"

"The men are sparsely placed. They encircle the town, yes, but their scant numbers mean we can break through wherever we choose. Only on the main road in from San Marco do they have any strength. They have a machine gun covering the entrance to town, but they have only one man every hundred yards around the rest."

The general nodded, his eyes narrow. "They are gearing up for a frontal attack. With so few men, they have little choice. When we hit one position, they will send reinforcements, leaving a hole in their defense. God is with us today, Lieutenant."

"Yes he *is*, sir! Orders?"

Chernitz left the car, finally, to join Lopez and Hernandez by the truck. Lopez smiled, barely short of open contempt, as the leery-looking gunrunner approached.

"Now," the general said, "we will have the opportunity to field-test your weapons, Emile."

Chernitz frowned. "Are you certain that this is the proper time, General? Might not this inflame your citizens even more?"

Lopez shook his head. "They will be so pleased that the rebellion has been stopped, they will give little thought to the how of it."

Chernitz nodded and offered no further comment.

To Hernandez, the general said, "Send a tank and ten men in on the main road. Obliterate the machine gun."

"Yes, sir."

"I want the other tank to circle the town and come in from the west, opposite us, with another ten men. That will draw Ansalmo's forces to that side of town."

"Yes, sir," Hernandez said. "That, uh, leaves only five men, sir."

"That's right," Lopez said. "Five men who will turn this fight in our favor . . . and who make this a historic day in the history of modern warfare."

"I don't understand, sir," Hernandez said.

Patiently, as if to a slow child, the general said, "In back of the truck there is a false bottom, Lieutenant—inside, you will find five new rifles. You know which men to give them to, correct?"

Hernandez nodded.

"Go! I want the attack to begin in ten minutes!"

"*Sí, mi general!*" Hernandez said, snapping off a salute and trotting away.

Chernitz trailing him, Lopez returned to his car, opened the trunk, and removed two AK–47s. He held one out to the arms dealer.

But Chernitz just stood there, hands limp at his sides. "I'm sorry, General, I only *sell* them—I don't use them."

"You are schooled in the demonstration of such weapons, am I not correct?"

"Yes, General, but—"

"Then you have a choice." Lopez cast a malevolent smile upon the gunrunner. "You can use one of these on our enemies . . . or I will use one of them on *you*. Emile, my friend, it is up to you."

Chernitz paled to the color of wet newspaper.

"In our country, Emile," Lopez said philosophically, "if you want to make money, you must *earn* it."

And he handed a gun to Chernitz.

For a man whose business was guns, Chernitz appeared supremely awkward, holding the AK–47.

"It won't bite you, Emile," the general assured his associate, thinking, *But then—it just might.*

Duke stepped out of the church, with Ansalmo, Romero, and Rojas with his bodyguard just behind him. The sun was bright in an impossibly blue sky; though this was autumn in Ciudad Pacífica, the humidity remained high, the temperature over eighty, with noon hours away. The town was long since up and moving about, people on sidewalks, cars driving past the church, children walking to school— just another day in this San Sebastiaoan hamlet.

Then, breaking the peaceful spell, came the distant rattle of a machine gun.

Bergman, Duke thought.

Turning instantly toward Rojas and Ansalmo, he yelled, "Back into the church! *Now*!"

Both men hesitated, but Rojas's bodyguard, plus another who'd been waiting outside, swept up the two men and rushed back inside.

Duke could hear AK–47s, and knew that Bergman had drawn return fire—he hoped that the *Guardia Nacional* men would hold their positions during the next fifteen minutes. By then, the battle would have been decided. . . .

Looking to his right, he saw Ripcord bursting from a building across the street, waving children toward cover, an empty gesture in a sleepy town that had been wakened before by visits from General Lopez. These people knew the drill, were already scurrying out of sight, cars suddenly speeding away from the gunfire, kicking up gravel.

Rip gave Duke a look and they both sprinted toward Bergman's position. As he ran, passing adobe buildings and cowering citizens, Duke was already playing out the possibilities, like a series of short films flashing on the movie screen of his mind. Each told him that this was a diversion—Lopez was merely rattling his saber, and this wasn't where the main thrust of his strike would come.

"Stop!" Duke yelled.

Rip skidded to a halt and spun in Duke's direction. "What up?"

"Diversion!"

Before he could explain further, shots rang out to their left. Duke heard M16s *and* AK–47s, and realized both sides were exchanging fire, now—Lopez attacking on two sides!

If that was it, they might be able to hold him off, for a while anyway. If Lopez had enough men to come from a third side, or if he had brought in armor, the good guys were in deep brown waters. . . .

As if on cue, the first shell lobbed in from the west, where the gunfire had just erupted, and Duke knew Lopez had armor even before the shell exploded beyond Ripcord, obliterating a small shed near an adobe house. Rip ducked, rolled, and came up running toward Duke.

The next shell came from the main road, to the north, and fell short of them, exploding in the street, sending up a cloud of dust and chunks of dirt that blew for yards in either direction, the shock wave almost knocking Duke off his feet.

Rip finally got to him. "He's got tanks."

"He's got tanks," Duke said.

They could hear gunfire from both directions.

Ripcord said, "Maybe we should put in for a transfer."

"Transfer?"

"Yeah, I was thinking maybe the Navy. What do you think? I like boats—you like boats? And we can both swim, right?"

"I hope so," Duke said. " 'Cause we're up the creek now, and I don't see a paddle. . . ."

Reports from the two tanks told Lopez what he already knew, hearing the sounds of battle: His troops had engaged Ansalmo's men.

Creeping through the jungle, Lopez, his five men, and Chernitz struggling to keep up in the rear, were still nearly a full kilometer from town, picking their way through the thick undergrowth.

Though it was taking longer than Lopez had planned, this wasn't such a bad thing—the longer he took, the more Ansalmo would believe he was dealing with only a two-pronged attack.

When Lopez and the pulse rifles arrived, it would be like shooting ducks on a pond.

*   *   *

Via coded text, Snake Eyes had let Gung Ho know that General Lopez was preparing to unleash the pulse weapons on Ciudad Pacífica.

With Snake Eyes pitching in, Gung Ho felt confident he and Heavy Duty could take care of their objective first, and stop the pulse weapons.

Before Heavy Duty, Gung Ho, and Snake Eyes followed Lopez and his men into the jungle, the unit leader considered bringing Scarlett along, but decided against it, when he heard the distant approach of Apache copters.

The Americans' hands would be full with Lopez's soldiers, not to mention tanks; but they would just have to deal with that. Gung Ho knew if he and the other JOEs didn't stop the pulse weapons, the rest wouldn't matter, anyway.

As the first Apache flew over, barely above the treetops, rustling leaves like a bad storm passing through, Gung Ho prayed Scarlett, on her own, would be able to stop them.

For the first time, he wondered if maybe they had erred, bringing in so small a unit when more soldiers could have made a real difference.

Even for G.I. JOEs, this one was a tall task. . . .

When she first heard the Apaches, Scarlett O'Hara smiled as if an old friend had shown up at her doorstep. Or make that, over her doorstep . . . *way* over. . . .

She had been hungering for action and, now, here it was . . . and she was ready.

Three Apaches on the horizon.

As the choppers neared, she made her move.

While the first one was still in front of her, she readied her crossbow pistol, fitting it with an explosive-tipped bolt. She aimed and, just when the first Apache was about to pass on her left, she fired.

Scant seconds later, the bolt struck the helicopter on the pilot's side, just below the rotor, making a small spark when the explosive detonated, followed by a moment so endless that Scarlett almost wondered if the bolt had done its job.

Almost.

Smoke erupted from the helicopter, the motor pitch changing from smooth to rough, then the chopper pitched hard right and, as the machine turned its belly to her like a frog on its back, she got just a glimpse of the pilot battling to control the helicopter before it fell from the sky and exploded in a huge fireball, like a sun setting just outside the peaceful hamlet.

The death of a fellow combatant never cheered her, but the success of her aim would save countless lives, and that did.

Case in point: The other two choppers were strafing the town, machine guns ripping into streets and buildings. Like big deadly birds of prey, the metal ships flew over, turned around, and just for good measure, strafed the town again.

But when they flew back over Scarlett's position, she was primed. . . .

The first bolt was loosed and, before it reached its target, Scarlett was already loading another explosive-tipped bolt. Her arrow struck the second chopper, this one hitting its tail rotor, spinning the machine and sending it crashing to an explosive finale on the jungle floor.

As the third Apache turned back toward the town, Scarlett followed its path, crossbow at the ready. When the shot came, her bolt flew straight, crashed through the Apache's windshield, and hit the pilot in the chest, killing him, and the copter's chances.

The chopper dropped dramatically, skipping off treetops as the copilot fought for control, but too late. After scraping through several trees, a wheel caught in the branches of one and the chopper was yanked from the blue. The craft shattered on impact, the clang of twisting metal echoing through the jungle like the howl of a giant, dying beast.

The explosion didn't come until almost ten seconds later, putting the beast out of its agony.

The redhead's smile was faint, but it was a smile—relishing the lives she had just saved, not those she had taken.

In the jungle that encroached upon the west side of town, Snake Eyes crept in behind a group of ten soldiers led by a lieutenant; they were, in turn, following a tank. The jungle here was too thick for his weapon of choice, the katana blade, and if he opened up with his machine gun, there were simply too many for him to get them all.

The first, a stoop-shouldered straggler, stopped and finally stood up straight, thanks to the knife that had struck him between the shoulder blades. For a few agonizing seconds, the man tried to reach around and pull the knife free, as if seeking to scratch an itch he couldn't reach, which he couldn't: He sank to his knees, then died without even toppling, a dead man praying.

The next two fell—one to a throwing star, another to a knockout blow from Snake Eyes's nunchakus. But the group he'd been thinning was nearing the friendlies' perimeter now, and Snake Eyes had to back off or risk being seen.

He would circle around to join Gung Ho and Heavy Duty on the side of town where the pulse weapons were coming in.

Explosions rocked the earth in and around Ciudad Pacífica, and Duke and Rip fought to maintain their balance as the ground shook under their feet.

"Man, I'm gettin' seasick!" Ripcord blurted.

"Then you better rethink the Navy, bro. Ships roll like this all the time. Motion of the ocean."

"I'm more Air Force material, anyway," Rip said.

Ansalmo, Rojas, and the two bodyguards exited the church and joined the duo, half a dozen armed men coming from nearby buildings to fall in.

"Damnit," Duke shouted over the battle roar, "I thought I told you two to stay in that church!"

Ansalmo stepped forward. "This is *our* country, Duke, and our *battle*. We cannot stand idly by, much less take sanctuary in a church, while you fight our battle for us. We will do our part, at your side."

Duke shook his head. "All right. But you two big shots better be prepared to take orders." He pointed. "Rip and I are going this way."

"And so shall we," Rojas said.

"No," Duke said. He pointed to the east. "You and your men need to defend *that* side. If this is a secondary diversion, we have barely any defense over there."

With a nod from Ansalmo, the two leaders and their men took off where Duke had indicated.

Duke hoped that by sending them away from the fighting, he could allow them to hold on to their honor and still avoid the central conflict. On the other hand, if Lopez had troops over there, Duke might well have just sent the only men who could save this country to their deaths—after all, other than the sniper Peters, the defense was damn thin.

Duke nodded to Rip and they took off, sprinting through the streets of Ciudad Pacífica and heading for the west.

Duke figured Bergman, on the road, would have his hands full, with a tank bearing down on him, but he would just have to hold out awhile longer—Duke and Rip had business on the west side.

So far, the defense there was holding up well. They were keeping the enemy at bay, though the tank was forging its way through the jungle, bearing down on the town.

Duke yelled, "We have *got* to take out that tank!"

Ripcord nodded, and sprinted to the right, dodging the tank's machine guns as he sought cover in the jungle. The big rumbling armored vehicle continued to lumber forward, crushing trees, plants, and anything else that crossed its path.

Duke tore to the left, spraying with machine-gun

fire the infantry behind the tank. Duke and Rip circled back, still firing at the infantry as they dove for cover. Duke was surprised—with their lieutenant, he counted only five men. He had taken two out already, so how many had his team and the *Guardia* guys knocked off before he and Rip got there?

The pair climbed aboard the tank from in back and made their way to the main hatch atop the vehicle, where Ripcord kept firing at the infantry to force their heads down while Duke spun the wheel to unlock the hatch.

As Duke flung it open, Rip used his teeth to pull the pin from a grenade, then dropped it inside. Duke slammed the hatch lid and both men dove to the ground on opposite sides.

Just as Duke hit, the ground seemed to jump up to meet him again with the explosion, though muffled by the tank, still loud enough to leave his ears ringing.

Smoke poured from the jagged aperture where the hatch had been, as well as from every crevice, fire crackling as the vehicle ground to a halt, a grotesque music box winding down. Duke heard a single awful scream from within, then silence.

With the destruction of the tank, the enemy soldiers cut and ran back into the jungle, members of Able Team and Ansalmo's machine gun–toting monks giving chase.

Duke and Ripcord joined pursuit, but it was Rip who caught up to Lieutenant Hernandez.

"Freeze!" Rip yelled, firing a burst into the air.

Hernandez stopped, his AK–47 dropping to the

ground next to him. The lieutenant wheeled, his face a mass of fear, recognizing his old "friend" from outside the bar.

"Interesting kinda support," Rip said, his gun trained on the lieutenant's gut, which not so long ago he'd sunk a boot into, "you and your general provide."

Hernandez's fear turned to rage. He cursed at Rip in Spanish and reached down to pull a bowie knife out of a scabbard strapped to his leg.

"Kill me where I stand, *maricón,* or fight me like a man! *You* choose."

A few yards away, Duke's attention shifted from his men taking soldiers prisoner to the showdown between Rip and Hernandez.

Duke yelled, "Do what he says—shoot him where he stands!"

But Rip let his M16 slip to the ground.

Duke hated it when his pal did this kind of thing. But he also knew Hernandez was going to hate it even more. . . .

Eyes narrowing, teeth bared, Hernandez rushed Rip, who sidestepped the blade and, as Hernandez shot past him, gave him a hard knife-edge to the back of the neck. The lieutenant tumbled ass over teakettle, but managed to come up with the blade still in hand, his eyes filled with even more hate.

Slowing his attack, Hernandez circled, the knife darting out occasionally, like crisp right jabs. On one lunge, Rip slapped Hernandez's knife arm out of the way and came over the top with a right that started at his shoes, then connected with his opponent's nose, making a nasty mushing noise, like a watermelon breaking on concrete.

Blood spurted from Hernandez's shattered nose and he howled like a wounded animal as he fell to his knees.

Bouncing on his toes, Rip said, "Float like a butterfly, sting like a—"

Hernandez lunged at Rip, the knife extended. As Hernandez's hand came up, Rip's foot came even faster, kicking the blade out of the lieutenant's hand, the blade tumbling end over end.

Hernandez jumped back, shaking his hand in pain even as he got to his feet. Rip caught the knife and spun away as Hernandez charged past. The lieutenant wheeled and roared back, an angry bull, but the matador was ready and jammed the blade into Hernandez's chest.

Hernandez blew out a long breath that might have been air escaping from a balloon. His eyes wide with shock, he slumped slowly to the ground, and died.

"Are you done screwing around?" Duke asked.

Rip nodded. "Suppose we oughta go get that other tank."

"You think?"

Gung Ho and Heavy Duty had caught up with the five soldiers accompanying General Lopez and the civilian gunrunner. The soldiers carried what were clearly the vaguely futuristic pulse rifles, sleek weapons with long, plump barrels. Lopez led the way, his men well behind him, the gunrunner lagging behind several yards.

When Gung Ho jack-in-the-boxed out of the undergrowth in front of Chernitz, the man almost fainted. The AK practically leapt out of his hands, as he threw up his arms.

At least the guy hadn't screamed like a frightened child—that kept a firefight from immediately erupting. Taking one step forward, Gung Ho locked eyes with the arms dealer.

"I *know* things," the guy blurted. "Don't kill me, please, don't kill me! I'm *valuable*. . . ."

Gung Ho smacked the sucker, knocking him cold as a dead carp, and used a plastic tie to bind the guy's hands behind him and bind his feet. What a waste of skin this jackass was.

Heavy Duty kept moving and caught up with a soldier. Using his silenced pistol, he shot the man in the head, watched him drop, then kept moving, as inexorable as death itself.

Snake Eyes came in from the flank and used his katana to separate one of the soldiers from his head, shooting a festive red geyser high into the green jungle.

Meanwhile, Gung Ho used his own silenced pistol to take out number three of the quintet.

Snake Eyes took out number four with a throwing star, while Heavy D got number five with a brutal knife-edge blow to the man's throat, dropping him to gurgle and die.

The three JOEs paused to silently watch as, up ahead, an oblivious Lopez kept moving through the jungle toward his target, now utterly alone, and unaware.

Soon he lacked even his G.I. JOE chaperones, who were busy gathering the next-generation rifles.

Duke and Ripcord got to the tank just as it rumbled into the north end of town. Bergman's hiding place had been blown to hell, though not necessarily Bergman himself. Others of his team and the *Guardia Nacional* men were keeping the small infantry group pinned down. This had obviously been a diversion, and couldn't have involved more than a dozen of Lopez's troops. There were certainly fewer now.

The plan was to attack this tank in the same way as the last. They climbed its sides toward the rear, and on top, Duke saw a Lopez soldier getting brave and preparing to take a shot at them with his AK–47.

Duke dove over the turret, tackling Ripcord as bullets from the AK raked across the tank. The two tumbled off and hit with a hard *thud* in the dirt road.

The shooter continued to fire until a monk shot him, small pink clouds bursting front and back as the bullet passed through.

Duke stayed down for a minute or so, taking inventory. Everything hurt, after he slammed into the road. Next to him, Ripcord had a small cut over one eyebrow, but otherwise looked okay.

"Ready to try again?" Duke asked.

"Born ready, Sergeant Rock—*go!*"

The two scrambled after the lumbering vehicle and climbed the thing again, opening the hatch and each pitching in a grenade; then, for the second time in less than five minutes, the duo dove off a tank.

They had no sooner hit the ground than the two grenades exploded, *boom boom*!

The tank creaked to a stop and again fire and smoke belched from where the top hatch had been. No screaming this time, at least.

After that, the San Sebastiaoan regulars tried to run away, but they were rounded up by the *Guardia* and guys from Able Team.

Duke's only concern now was the east side. They had fought battles on the west and north, as well as the road that ran in and out the south end of town. He wondered if Lopez could have sent his men, without coming himself. They had either killed or scooped up most of Lopez's people, but had not seen (much less found) the general.

Duke and Rip took off for the east side, where the hamlet and the jungle melted together in a blurry border.

They got to the last building and saw no sign of their defense—neither Ansalmo, Rojas, nor any of the rebels. A path yawned into the jungle, but instead of taking it, Duke and Rip cut through on either side.

They heard nothing, but as he crept along, gun ready, Duke thought he saw the foliage rustling ahead. As they closed the distance, Duke realized they were coming up behind Ansalmo, Rojas, and the two bodyguards.

Duke whistled softly, the bodyguards wheeling, and he waved to make sure they wouldn't shoot him and Rip. The odds he'd one day die in battle were good, but Duke would be damned if he'd go out by friendly fire. Scanning swiftly around the treetops, Duke sought a sign of the sniper Peters, but as usual, the man was invisible.

Moving up, Duke knelt next to Ansalmo. "Anything?"

The president shook his head. "Someone's out there, but I haven't heard much noise. They're either very quiet, or only a few are left."

"We'll go have a look," Duke said.

He and Rip slipped forward, crawling low, listening carefully. They were twenty yards from Ansalmo and Rojas when Duke peeked between leaves and saw General Lopez standing alone just off the path, his back to Duke, AK–47 hanging slack in one hand.

Behind Lopez was a bloody trail of his own dead soldiers, as yet unnoticed by the general. Obviously, Peters had been busy.

Duke lined Lopez up in his sights and rose.

Before he could say anything, Ansalmo said, "General Lopez, you are under arrest for treason. Drop your weapon."

Duke's attention was drawn to Ansalmo, but he still saw the general lift his AK and spin. Duke spun, too, sending a bullet into the general's forehead, giving him a third, slightly higher, eye. This third eye, however, would unlikely bring enlightenment to its late bearer. . . .

The sniper, Peters, came up behind them. "What the hell *happened* here, Duke?"

Looking at Peters, Duke asked, "*You* didn't do this?"

Peters pointed at one dead soldier, a throwing star protruding from the man's back. "Since when do snipers use those babies?"

Rip essayed the bodies. "Where the hell are their guns? What, were they gonna beat us to death with palm fronds?"

Turning to the others, Duke asked, "Señor Rojas, is this the work of your men?"

Rojas shook his head. "My men use only firearms."

The group walked farther into the jungle and found three more bodies and, beyond them, a lone AK–47 lying in the grass.

Turning to Rip, Duke asked, "What the hell happened here?"

Looking out into the jungle, Rip said, "I have no idea. And you know what? I don't give a damn, 'cause the good guys won."

They turned back to see Rojas and Ansalmo shaking hands and smiling.

With a little shrug, Duke said, "Maybe that's enough for today. Hell, maybe it's enough for any day. The good guys won, and let's leave it at that."

CHAPTER TEN

Objective: Su Loc

Undisclosed Location

Those working at the secret detention facility in a G.I. JOE member nation knew an authorized team was using a cell on the base, within the block used to detain terrorists, but the staff did not know who they were or why they were there. The black fatigues of the G.I. JOE unit probably convinced the guards that they were either CIA or private contractors, although Snake Eyes's ninja outfit did raise some brows.

Right now, Snake Eyes and Heavy Duty were stationed outside the interview room door. Gung Ho and Scarlett were with their prisoner in the spartan room, whose dull green walls seemed to soak up the fluorescent overheads. Breaker sat in an adjacent observation room, manning communications gear that would allow a video hookup between here and the Pit, where General Hawk would conduct the questioning via the video feed.

Their prisoner had been identified by Hawk as Emile Chernitz, though they'd already known that, G.I. JOE having tracked the dealer and his pulse weapons since the rifles had left the Uzekurkistan complex, which had been destroyed by the U.S. insertion team.

The recovered scientists were back under the watchful eye of NATO, and that meant—for now at least—the five futuristic pulse rifles in the possession of Unit Alpha were the only ones known to have reached a buyer.

More than one truck had left the complex, however, and Gung Ho knew what those vehicles carried would be high on Hawk's priority list.

Positioned by a flat-screen monitor with a mini-camera attached, waiting for Breaker to make the final connection, Gung Ho glanced over at their prisoner.

Emile Chernitz, in an orange jumpsuit and flip-flops, sat in a straight-back chair, hands prayerfully on the table, the chain from his cuffs threaded through a metal welded loop. Chernitz didn't look much worse for the wear, but for a puffy black eye courtesy of Gung Ho, who'd smacked him in the jungle.

Scarlett, standing behind the prisoner, was there for security purposes—the general and Gung Ho would handle the questioning.

"We're good to go," Breaker said over the intercom.

Gung Ho was careful to stay to one side of the screen and its Minicam.

A seated General Hawk appeared at his desk in his office at the Pit. He asked, "Everything running smoothly?"

Gung Ho turned to nod at the little camera

above the screen. "You greased the wheels just fine, sir—they gave us everything we asked for, no problem."

"Good," Hawk said. "Let's talk to our guest."

Gung Ho swiveled to Chernitz, whose dour countenance revealed no fear. The cowardice the gunrunner had displayed in the jungle seemed to have been left behind in San Sebastiao.

"I have nothing to say," Chernitz said, displaying a mirthless, cigarette-stained smile.

Casually, Gung Ho said, "I could've killed you in the jungle, remember. And people *have* been known to disappear at this facility."

Chernitz just kept the smile going, a crooked thing, like a painting not hanging right.

"Could've left you there to rot," Gung Ho said. "You were plenty talkative, then."

The gunrunner shrugged. "I will say nothing until I have been allowed to contact my country's embassy in Washington, D.C."

Leaning closer, his voice casual with menace, Gung Ho said, "Just because you aren't decomposing in the jungle right now, don't think your body couldn't mysteriously end back up there."

Chernitz flinched slightly, his eyes briefly touching the stare Gung Ho had locked on him.

Finally the smile faded. "You couldn't do that. Americans don't do those kinds of things."

"Said the prisoner in an undisclosed location. Anyway, we're not with the U.S. government."

"But . . . who . . . ?"

"We're nobody. We don't exist. And when you

don't exist, you don't have to play by any given set of rules."

Chernitz's fear caught back up with him. He said nothing, but Gung Ho could tell the man had taken the threat seriously—he'd been bluffing, of course, but the important thing was, Chernitz had bought it.

"Let's start with the trucks," Hawk said.

Chernitz addressed the flat screen. "What trucks?"

"We'll skip that step. What was *in* the trucks, Mr. Chernitz? Where did they go? Who has them now?"

Afraid or not, Chernitz was no fool. With a tiny grin, he said, "Pardon me for answering a question with a question . . . but should I decide to answer your inquiries, what would I win, on this game show of yours?"

"That would depend," Hawk said, "on your level of cooperation."

"Would I be released?"

"You would do some prison time, if for no other reason than your own protection."

"It seems I already *am* in prison."

Hawk's smile seemed genial. "Then I take it that facility is your new residence of choice?"

They all waited while the gunrunner digested that.

After a moment, Hawk said, "Let's start again. Where are the trucks now?"

"I do not know."

Gung Ho tilted his head and gave the gunrunner a look.

Cowering, Chernitz said, "You must believe me.

The entire shipment was not mine—I know only of the five cases that I purchased."

"Five?" Hawk asked.

Chernitz nodded. "Must I tell you that there are many people in my profession? Fifty cases were up for bid. I am a small procurement company—I could afford only ten percent of the weapons."

"How many rifles to the case?" Hawk asked.

"Five."

"So the weapons recovered in the San Sebastiaoan jungle comprise only one case. Where are your other four?"

"They have not been sold," Chernitz said, "I assure you. They are stored safely."

"Where?" Hawk demanded.

"In a warehouse . . . but more than that, I will not tell you—not until we have negotiated terms."

"Terms?"

The gunrunner nodded firmly. "I want out of here, and I want to avoid prison."

"I'll get you out of there," Hawk said, "but, Mr. Chernitz—you *are* going to spend many years in prison. Again, how many, and where, will depend on your level of cooperation."

Chernitz's expression mingled disappointment and indignation; so did his tone: "That does not sound like much, in exchange for such valuable information."

"Or," the general said affably, "you can spend the rest of your life in a prison in Uzekurkistan. You know how they feel about gunrunners there— a bullet in the back of the head appears to be the favored remedy. Now—it's up to you, but first understand, there *will* be prison. Either an unspecified time in an American one . . . or life—or perhaps death—in a Uzekurkistan one."

"There must be some other—"

"That ends our negotiation. Choose, Mr. Chernitz."

Chernitz bent down to wipe his sweaty face with a cuffed hand. Then he smiled in a sickly fashion.

"An American prison," he said.

"Good," Hawk said. Any geniality or affability disappeared from the general's expression. "Now answer the goddamn question—where are the other four cases?"

After emitting a long sigh of defeat, Chernitz said, "Manaus."

Gung Ho frowned. "Brazil?"

The gunrunner nodded. "The crates came up the Amazon that far, but I did not trust taking them all into San Sebastiao without a buyer. I put them in a warehouse in Manaus."

"Details," Gung Ho said.

Chernitz provided an address. "The crates are labeled 'agricultural equipment.' "

Scarlett spoke for the first time. "Why agricultural equipment?"

The gunrunner did not try to look at the woman, who was standing almost directly behind him. "It is a bad joke."

"Try me."

"As I said to General Lopez, 'You should see them plow up the earth.' "

"You're a riot, Chernitz," Gung Ho said.

Hawk said, "We'll have someone at that warehouse within an hour . . . and the guns better be where you say they are."

"They were safe when I left for San Sebastiao," the gunrunner insisted, "and I have a trusted man keeping watch."

Gung Ho frowned. "Your man—will he be a problem for our people?"

Chernitz shook his head. "No, no, no. You do not understand. Lopez, he did not understand either. We are *salesmen,* not soldiers. I would not have been in that jungle, except for that son of a whore Lopez! He threatened to kill me if I did not go with him."

Gung Ho leaned in and said, "If you really want out of this hellhole, you better tell me something I don't know."

"I *gave* you the guns! You didn't know where—"

"You made it easier, but we would have found them without you."

Chernitz shrugged. "Perhaps. But I doubt it. . . . If I could give you more, could you get me into minimum security? The country-club places where the American politicians and white-collar criminals go?"

Hawk said, "No guarantees. But your good will might go a long way."

But Chernitz just sat there, saying nothing.

Finally, Gung Ho said to Scarlett, "Let's pack it up. We're done here. This lowlife can rot here in limbo till hell freezes over."

Chernitz strained against his cuffs. "But . . . we had a *deal.* . . ."

"A deal?" Gung Ho's grin was as big as it was

nasty. "A deal like when you offered the pulse weapons to the rebels, then sold them at a higher price to Lopez, instead?"

"That was business."

"So is this. You want something from us, we want something in return. Just good business, right, Chernitz?"

The arms dealer considered this. He licked his lips, his fear replaced with nervousness. "There . . . there is *one* thing. I do not know the particulars, but I do know that there is a place where the most brilliant scientists on this earth, they are developing super soldiers."

Gung Ho laughed. "Super my achin'—"

"No! *Not* your aching *anything*!" Chernitz was pleading for understanding now. "These top brains are working on a way to nullify soldiers' fear sensor, their pain sensors, too. Within a very short time, they will be creating soldiers with no fear of death, and with no pain threshold *whatsoever*. The old expression, fight to the death? This they will do."

A skeptical Gung Ho sneaked a peek at the general on the flat screen; but the general seemed to be taking Chernitz seriously.

Hawk asked, "Where are these experiments being run?"

"In Eandok. A village called Su Loc. Scientists are at work there now. They have been working on this project for years, the location moving from time to time. They are close."

Hawk said, "Gung Ho, leave him—"

"What?" Chernitz bellowed.

"Allow me to finish, Mr. Chernitz," Hawk said pleasantly. "Leave him there, and I'll get the Navy to make the transfer to a U.S. prison."

Chernitz sighed; he was trembling with relief.

Hawk was saying to Gung Ho, "You and your team get on the plane I'm sending and haul butt back here now. You have another mission."

Washington, D.C.

Duke Hauser was scared spitless.

Combat? No problem. HALO jump from thirty thousand feet? Piece of cake. Facing Ana tonight? Terrifying.

This was to be their special night, and he wanted everything to be perfect. After the way he'd left her in the lurch when the San Sebastiao mission came along, he had some serious making up to do.

He had wrangled four tickets to a swank military dance, and had already decided tonight would be the night—now or never, or anyway it felt like that, with the team shipping out again in the morning.

Information they'd gathered in San Sebastiao had made HQ decide something needed to be done about the so-called super soldier experiments. Able Team had been elected to perform a recon and destruction of the facility. Intel had learned of a village called Su Loc in the Asian country of Eandok. That was their destination tomorrow. But tonight? That was a whole other mission.

Once again he and Ripcord sat at a table in Tom and Harvey's Steak House, surrounded by diners and tuxedo-shirt clad servers, the din of the restaurant a murmur at this early hour. Decked out in their dress uniforms, the pair drew the eyes of many, including a good share of attractive women, and even though Rip flirted openly with several, Duke concerned himself only with the one who'd yet to arrive.

As they waited for Ana and Rex, each nursed a drink, a dirty martini for Rip, Diet Coke for Duke, who wanted his wits about him on this special night.

They had just emptied their glasses when Ana and Rex entered, the major in his dress uniform, Ana in a black gown, her blonde hair perfect. As brother and sister crossed the restaurant, all eyes turned, but few studied the scientist, the majority fixed on the stunning blonde, who glided to their table, her smile effervescent.

"I'm so glad you're back safe," she said.

"And am I glad to *be* back," Duke said, and slipped his arms around her.

She kissed Duke chastely as Rex and Rip shook hands. Then they exchanged places, Ana planting one on Rip's cheek while Rex and Duke gave each other a quick hug and handshake.

The four sat down, Ana to Duke's right, the couple holding hands. Rex sat next to his sister on the other side, and Ripcord on Duke's left.

Rex ordered a bottle of wine, which he of course had to taste before the others were allowed to sample it. They ordered dinner, then the quartet made small talk before Rex said, "I've got an announcement to make."

They turned to him, Duke wondering what this was about.

Raising his glass, Rex said, "I'd like to offer up a toast to . . . well . . . myself."

They all gave him quizzical, even goofy looks, but raised their glasses.

Rex gave them his trademark boyish smile. "I got the news from General Robertson just an hour ago. I finally get to go into the field. I'll be joining Able Team on this mission."

Duke's eyes cut to Ana, whose shock was obvious.

Not that he wasn't stunned, too. No one had yet told him Rex was joining the team. They already had a medical officer, so Rex's presence must mean something else. Then again, their final briefing wouldn't be until right before they left.

"So," Rex said, "here's to me, *soldier*-scientist, not just scientist."

Rip and Duke clinked glasses with the ecstatic young major. His sister clinked her glass, too, though coming in late, as the other three were about to withdraw theirs.

"C-c-congratulations, Rex," she managed, her voice tight with emotion. "I know you've wanted this for a long, long time."

Rip said, "Way to *go*, man!" He shook hands with their friend again. "I *knew* you weren't any average, ordinary lab rat."

"No, I'm an extraordinary lab rat."

"Ha! Can't wait to see how you hold up, out in the field with the big boys."

While Rip and Rex bantered, Duke watched the

woman he loved; from her expression, she might have just heard her brother confess a terminal illness. Tears welled but seemed unable to fall. Duke rested a hand on hers and she squeezed hard enough to make him give up government secrets.

The others finally noticed her tension, and Rex locked eyes with his sister. "Ana, darling . . . it'll be okay. This is what I *want*."

"I know, I know," she said. "I'm just happy for you."

After dinner, they went to the dance, a black-tie fund-raising event to help support the families of military people serving in war zones overseas. Considering Rex's declaration at dinner, what had seemed the perfect evening for Duke and Ana now took on, for him, an unsettling edge.

The crowd was mostly military people, officers and enlisted men together with their spouses and dates, a live orchestra playing romantic, if somewhat old-fashioned music.

The women were gorgeous, but none compared by even half to Ana. As they moved gracefully around a dance floor aswirl with colorful gowns, Duke proved surprisingly light on his feet.

Ana smiled up at him. "Where did you learn to dance like this?"

"Lessons when I was a kid . . . but if you tell Rip, I'll deny it."

She looked past him. "He's trying out a few moves himself."

Ripcord, at a floorside table, was downing shots with a quartet of enlisted women.

He whispered to her: "That looks a little ambitious even for Rip, don't you think?"

Her laugh was musical. "Let's not tell him that the one next to him is General Murphy's daughter."

"Let's not."

As they danced by his table, they could hear Rip saying, "Ladies, my hot tub holds four, easy. . . . Five with a little effort."

They were still laughing at that when Duke led Ana outside onto a quiet verandah, where a handful of tables awaited them, couples seated romantically here and there. One table was free, and they took it. The lights of Washington shimmered beyond them like a jewel box had been emptied into the night.

Speaking of jewels. . . .

Suddenly, dramatically, he knelt before her like a knight to his lady. He displayed the small box, open to reveal the very respectably sized diamond engagement ring—this was a mission he had carefully planned and was now flawlessly executing.

Ana gasped with shock and joy, her eyes as bright as the diamond she was regarding.

Shyly, he said, "I've been wanting to do this before we deploy."

"Duke . . . it's beautiful. It's *too* nice, you wonderful lunatic."

He slipped back into his chair, and said, "Only time I'll ever be buyin' one of these, so why not splurge a little?"

They stared into each other's faces, and the moment was a lovely one . . . at least until Duke realized he hadn't actually gotten an answer out of her yet.

"Well, baby. . . . What do you say?"

She was trying to say something, but her emotions were clogging the way.

From behind them they heard a very familiar voice say: "Say *yes,* you idiot girl. Don't you know a real American Hero when you see one?"

Rex sauntered up, obviously happy for them.

Kneeling by their table, with one hand on Duke's shoulder and the other on his sister's, Rex said, "You better say yes, before I spill the state secrets to my prospective brother-in-law . . . like what it's like to share a damn *bathroom* with you."

"Rex," Duke said, with a grin, "you do know how to kill a mood."

"Sorry, buddy. I was just coming over to offer you a ride back to the post."

Ana frowned. "It's that time already?"

Duke half smiled. "We go at oh-five-hundred."

"Is it . . . ?" She frowned. "It *is,* right? You're going. That's why you're pulling Rex out of the lab to—"

"Ana," Duke said, "you know we can't say—"

"Yes, I know, yes, yes. Classified. Top secret. You'd have to kill me if you told me, blah, blah, blah."

He chuckled. "Well, speaking of classified information . . . you still haven't given me an answer."

"Yes!" The big blue eyes popped. "Of course, it's yes."

He let out a relieved sigh, but the tip of her forefinger came to his lips.

"One condition, big boy. . . ."

She grabbed Rex and pulled him over. "Promise me you won't let my genius brother get hurt." Her eyes went to Rex, and the love there was unmistakable. "This little egghead is the only family I have left." And now her eyes traveled to her fiancé. "*Promise* me. . . ."

"I promise," he said.

Her smile was a trembling thing, a leaf in a breeze, as she held out her hand and allowed him to thread the ring onto the proper finger. Rex took this in with a smile, though his eyes hinted at the loss he felt, his sister's love promised to another man.

Behind them came a shatter of glass, and a figure crashed to the brick floor of the verandah, near the trio—Rip, arms and legs akimbo, had joined the little group.

Duke said, "Jesus, Rip! Are you making an entrance or an exit?"

Rip ignored this, checking his jaw to see if it still worked after the blow he'd received that had sent him flying onto the verandah.

He yelled back into the main room: "Your damn *hand* is gonna feel that, in the morning!"

Still on the floor, Rip glanced up at his friends, nodded hello, then noticed the ritual in progress. "Hey, man, nice rock! You finally proposing to this girl?"

"I'm done proposing," Duke said.

"And I already said yes," Ana said.

"Well," Rip said, "it ain't official till you answer *my* question. Do you love my main man?"

"With all my heart. Always and forever."

Pulling out his cellphone, Rip snapped a picture of the happy couple. Then, studying it, he said, "Looks like now I've gotta find somebody to love *me* . . ." He got up and headed back in. ". . . starting in my hot tub, for as many times as possible in the next three hours. . . ."

Duke, Ana, and Rex shared laughter at their off-the-wall friend. Despite Rex's news that had so unsettled his sister, the evening had turned out perfect after all.

The C–130 had a service ceiling of thirty-three thousand feet, and though they cruised at only about 85 percent of that total, breathing was still impossible without bottled oxygen. The back door hung open, the roar of air rushing past indiscernible from that of the engines—just one huge blast to Gung Ho. The HALO jump was a dangerous undertaking, but entering Eandok undetected was imperative, making jumping the best option.

In back were the other members of Unit Alpha—Snake Eyes, Heavy Duty, Scarlett, and Breaker; their leader's eyes were glued to the two vertically aligned lights, one red and one green. The red one was on, and he waited for the green.

They were dressed in insulated black jumpsuits, protection from the cold at this altitude, plus black crash helmets with face shields, oxygen tanks, and breathing masks, as well as the usual mission gear and weapons.

Gung Ho's stomach was tight, though not with fear—just a simple case of nerves, same as at the beginning of any mission. The waiting, as Tom Petty said, was the hardest part.

The mission, this time, was much the same as the South American one: Get to the objective, destroy it, get the hell out, and remain invisible all the way. Once again, the Americans would be on the scene—the able Able Team in fact, and with the same objective as G.I. JOE, at least superficially.

But General Hawk had told Gung Ho, and Gung Ho only, that the super-soldier lab must be destroyed before the Americans could send their own scientist in to obtain the research.

G.I. JOE's goal was to help maintain balance—no new world order could be allowed to take hold. The Americans, however well-meaning, had no more business with this deadly new technology than a rogue state or arms manufacturer or international criminal organization.

Eandok was a small Asian country, sandwiched lengthwise between Thailand on the west and Cambodia on the east. Under the rule of a military tribunal—which maintained power through a policy of killing anyone who stood up to them—the country had been isolationist since the three generals had taken control just after the beginning of the new millennium.

The village that was the JOE unit's objective, Su Loc, rested in what was known as the highlands of Eandok. From this height, however, nothing seemed high except the airplane itself—nothing to see below them but clouds in the dark night sky.

The light turned green.

"Go!" Gung Ho yelled.

Snake Eyes went first, Heavy Duty right behind him, then Scarlett, then Breaker, and finally the team leader.

The roar lessened little as Gung Ho plummeted earthward—felt as though the wind was trying to tear his head off. Swooping, enjoying the exhilaration of the jump, Gung Ho caught patchy glimpses of green earth, probably a good four miles below.

Hands at his side, feet tight together, Gung Ho rocketed downward, the team fanned out beneath him, all racing down too, in their own patches of air.

The fall to the thirty-five-hundred-foot level, where he would open the chute, took less than two minutes at terminal velocity—one hundred twenty-six miles per hour.

Around him, team members shot up past him as their chutes opened and they were jolted briefly skyward. When he hit the magic mark, Gung Ho yanked his ripcord—as the chute opened and filled with air, he felt as though his arms were being jerked off at the shoulders.

He guided his chute by pulling the toggles, hitting within a few feet of his team, rolling, and coming up unhitching the parachute and wrapping it up into a ball.

Heavy Duty had already started digging a hole and Snake Eyes and Gung Ho pitched in. When it was large enough, each dropped their chutes in, along with their oxygen tanks and jumpsuits. With the exception of Snake Eyes in his trademark black ninja garb, they were dressed now in the camouflage fatigues worn under the jumpsuits. Guns at the ready, they moved off into the jungle heading for checkpoint number one.

The military tribunal that ran the country was paranoid enough to run regular patrols through the countryside. Though the country was technically at peace, the danger level remained high for the G.I. JOE unit.

Snake Eyes, naturally, took point, with Heavy Duty on drag, the other three spaced between. The foliage was as thick as the undergrowth in San Sebastiao, and the humidity even worse. At least the mosquitoes were smaller. Of course, they had to be on the lookout for the fifty-one varieties of snakes indigenous to Eandok. The good news was, only forty-nine species were poisonous; the bad news was, the other two were boa constrictors.

Unit Alpha was halfway to checkpoint one when they came to a raging river that split the path before them.

Scarlett said, "Wasn't this a creek on the map at our briefing?"

"Roger that," Heavy Duty said. "And there was a *bridge*. . . ."

Gung Ho said, "Damn Mapquest, anyway."

That broke the tension, and they laughed.

All the intel—the pinhole satellites, GPS, assets on the ground, everything the various countries involved in G.I. JOE had to offer—would mean nothing if their mission came undone, courtesy of a rainstorm and flash flood.

"Monsoon season's cranking up early," Gung Ho said. "Storm left us this torrent, and took the bridge to hell and gone."

Scarlett asked, "You want Snake Eyes to search for another crossing?"

Gung Ho shook his head. "First thing we need to do is get off this path. We may not be the *only* ones who don't know the bridge is out."

They moved into the underbrush, found themselves a small clearing not far from the path, and gathered in a small circle. Getting out his map, Gung Ho risked shining his flashlight on it for thirty seconds, then killed the beam.

"There isn't a road for ten klicks either direction," he said. "That's why we landed in this area. Not very many people . . ."

"So," Heavy D said, "not very many roads."

"Not very many roads." He gave them all a look. "We're going to have to swim it."

They stared at him skeptically.

Breaker said, "No, seriously—"

"Seriously," Gung Ho said.

Eyeing the raging current, Scarlett said, "Got to be another way."

Gung Ho's wrist communicator vibrated and he looked down to see a text message from Snake Eyes: THERE IS.

Turning to the silent ninja, Gung Ho said, "If you've got a better idea, I'm all ears."

And using the wrist communicators, Snake Eyes outlined his plan.

Gung Ho liked it. Maybe only one JOE had to brave the rushing water without a safety line. Could work.

Nodding, Gung Ho said, "Good plan, but I'll go, not you."

Snake Eyes argued that the team leader should not take such a risk.

"You know better than that," Gung Ho said. "We're all equally important in my eyes and, anyway, RHIP. I'll go."

Rank did indeed have its privileges, but as Gung Ho tied the loop of rope round his waist, he secretly wanted nothing to do with this challenge. But he was not the sort of leader who'd give anyone a task he was unwilling to do himself.

Heavy Duty would hold one end of the rope and feed it out as Gung Ho swam across the swollen stream. If Gung Ho got in trouble, Heavy D was the strongest, and would have the best chance of reeling him back in.

Not a complex plan, but if it failed, their mission to Eandok might be over before it had really begun. . . .

With the rope secured around his waist, Gung Ho strode to the edge of the flooded creek, now a quarter-mile-wide torrent that would do its best to sweep him along with its racing current.

"Good luck," Scarlett said to him.

But it was Heavy D who said, "Thanks," adding, "I'll probably need it, to keep his Cajun behind from dragging me down to the Gulf of Thailand."

Gung Ho laughed and then so did the rest of Unit Alpha, loud enough to be heard over the raging water. They were a good group—not a slacker in the lot, and if this little swim kept them safe, Gung Ho didn't mind getting wet at all.

He jumped in, surprised by the cold, considering they were in a jungle where the temp was probably in the nineties. He waded only a step or two before the current became too strong, and he had to swim. He was trying to maintain a straight course, but it was impossible. The heavy current pushed him downstream far faster than he was making progress across.

Heavy Duty could find no way to help him with the rope, either—the line was not set up to allow Heavy D to guide him on a straight path. This was strictly one of those cords you pulled only in the case of emergency, though as he fought against being swept up by the current, Gung Ho wondered what it would take to turn this into *more* of an emergency. . . .

His muscles ached, and he was barely halfway across. He was already a good twenty yards downstream from where he had begun. The spot they'd picked for their crossing would allow Heavy D and the others to walk downstream with him for a while, and eventually running out of rope would become a real concern. . . .

Swimming harder now, feeling the river gaining the edge, Gung Ho pushed himself, reaching, pulling, each handful of water, each leg kick bringing him closer to both success and failure as the relentless wall of water and debris swept him away.

But even though his strength ebbed, he would not give up. Summoning one last kick, he swam headlong and finally reached the far side, having just enough strength left to pull himself out and land in an exhausted, soaking heap on the far shore.

As he tied the rope off to a huge palm tree, Gung Ho vowed that the next time Snake Eyes volunteered, he'd let the ninja have his way.

CHAPTER ELEVEN
Air Strike

Su Loc, Eandok

The Southeast Asian jungle was not new territory for Duke and Rip—they had been all over the world, after all—but this was their first trip to Eandok.

San Sebastiao had represented more of a spy mission—disguises, false identities, and the sort of James Bond stuff that Able Team had done occasionally, but that was not really in their comfort zone.

This mission, however, fell right in their wheelhouse, and Eandok being literally foreign territory bothered Duke not a whit. The team had landed in Thailand, taken a truck to near the border, and crossed at night as passengers in a low-flying Blackhawk helicopter.

Three team members had sustained what were considered major injuries on the South American mission—they would all be fine, but were not along for this ride. In addition, new medical officer Arturo Benitez had indeed been temporarily replaced by Rex Lewis, who would do double duty—

Rex had his own orders, to which Duke was not privy, regarding the scientific aspects of the mission.

This much Duke knew: If the super-soldier experiments were as real, and troublesome, as promised, Rex was the right choice to understand and interpret any information they gathered in Su Loc.

Instead of the usual ten-man team, Able Team's strength was seven, one unseasoned . . . in fact, Rex had never been in the field before.

The margin for error on this particular insertion was next to nothing. Able Team was the best, of that Duke was confident; but even a Super Bowl winner could look pretty pedestrian after racking up enough injuries and with a lineup littered with inexperienced players.

A bundle of flat-roofed buildings of either paint-peeling cement or flimsy corrugated metal added up to something between a town and a village, the landscape a crazy quilt of dead cars and garbage cans, which seemed to be the central decorating theme of Su Loc.

From the air, the only road looked like a narrow black snake—in most of the world, little more than a wagon trail; in Eandokian terms, the equivalent of an interstate. On a normal day, they might've been able to cross that "interstate" from Thailand to here. But the rain had left the road a ribbon of muck, and today Able Team would never have made it—not without running into a patrol, anyway.

The generals of Eandok made San Sebastiao's General Lopez seem like Mother Teresa's naughty nephew. All the land in the country was available for rent, the whole population for sale as slaves. An Eandokian citizen's best way to stay safe from the generals was joining the military that served them. Only soldiers got enough to eat, or had any kind of privileges, or any faint hope for the future. . . .

Wind whipped through the Blackhawk as Duke, Rip, and Rex sat three-wide on one side. Peters the sniper, Bergman and his M–60, and Stearns sat three-wide opposite. Between them, a rifleman named Edgerson perched cross-legged. An African American soldier from Brooklyn, New York, he'd grown up on streets rougher than some missions he'd been on since joining Able Team.

Despite their headsets, Rip had to yell to be heard over the roaring engine and the whistling wind. "I can't believe you're getting married."

Duke grinned. "Why not? Figure I was too smart to ever get hitched?"

"No! I thought Ana was too smart to ever say, 'yes.' "

"Mess with me if you like, buddy. But you're looking at a happy man."

"Would *I* mess with *you*?"

Rex joined in: "Never! Like *you* weren't messing with anybody last night, Rip—when you came flying out of that club?"

"Got that right, Rex my man—just minding my own business, havin' an intelligent conversation with those enlisted women."

"So, then," Duke said, "it wasn't General Murphy who knocked you through the window?"

Rip shook his head, moving his jaw to make sure

it still worked right. "His adjutant. Turns out he's dating the general's daughter, and figured I'd overstepped."

"Really?" Rex asked. "What were you doing?"

"We were havin' this innocent little contest about whether or not I could drink a shot of tequila without spilling it."

"Why did the adjutant hit you for that?"

"His girlfriend was holding the shot glass."

"So?"

"She wasn't usin' her hands." Rip smiled, nostalgic for the night before. "You know, I didn't spill a damn drop."

They were laughing when the pilot's voice came into their headsets.

"Five minutes until touchdown."

"Roger that," Duke said.

Once they'd made it across the swollen stream, Gung Ho gave the team "Take five" to recover, then pressed on, heading for checkpoint one, where they met their contact, an Eandokian national named Vin Sook.

Short, with stringy black hair, a narrow tan face, and random yellow teeth, Vin Sook looked unimpressive to say the least; nonetheless, he turned out to be plenty bright—he and his beat-up Toyota pickup had managed to successfully avoid government patrols for the last five hours.

Sometimes on the road, sometimes off, Vin Sook and his trusty truck brought Unit Alpha fifty klicks from checkpoint one, never once getting them caught or stuck in the brown glue that passed for roads.

Four JOEs rode in the rusty truck's bed, Gung Ho sharing the cab with their native guide. A small pass-through in the back window made conversation easier between Gung Ho and those in back.

"How much farther, Daddy?" Heavy Duty asked. "My butt is gettin' beat to hell!"

"What, a tough guy like you?" Gung Ho said.

Heavy D gave him a nasty smile. "Trade places with me, bro, and we'll *see* who's—"

"*Quiet!*" Vin Sook jumped in. "Patrol coming!"

The guide cranked the wheel hard left and the truck jumped off the road, into the jungle. The four teammates in back bounced like sacks of grain. Fifteen yards in, surrounded by high grass, Vin Sook slammed the brakes and killed the motor. Snake Eyes vaulted out and disappeared into the underbrush.

Thirty seconds later, Gung Ho's wrist communicator vibrated and he looked down to see a Morse code message from Snake Eyes: PATROL PASSING IN TRUCK.

"You get out now," Vin Sook said. "Su Loc, five kilometers that way." He pointed eastward. "You follow road, but stay in jungle. Patrol come back, one hour."

"Okay," Gung Ho said. He'd figured the guide would get them closer, but said nothing.

The guide picked up on that, and said, "If I drive you Su Loc, someone see me. They see me with *you,* I dead. You dead, too."

They could all relate to that. Collaborators took

great risks to aid the G.I. JOE team. No one held it against them when they reached their limit to help and still feel safe.

Something tripped in Gung Ho's mind. "You're not going to Su Loc, are you?"

Vin Sook shook his head. "I go other way. You will call in air strike . . . I die if I there."

Gung Ho asked, "How many people are there?"

"Civilians?"

"Yeah."

"None. They all gone."

Gung Ho felt sick to his stomach. "How many soldiers?"

"Two platoons."

It all made sense now.

Their intel had been sketchy. Word was, experiments on the super soldiers were going on in Su Loc, but no ID on the building used as a lab. Activity in several buildings had been noted, and Hawk had not wanted to bomb the whole town in order to take out a few madmen.

Hawk had wanted Unit Alpha to ID the right building, then call in an air strike, and before the Americans could get their scientist in—though Able Team planned to then take out the lab themselves, according to Hawk's intel.

But now Gung Ho had information the Americans didn't have. . . .

He knew why no one had been able to identify the building: The citizens had been evacuated or killed or God knew what, replaced by one hundred Eandokian regulars who, dressed as citizens, made the town look busy . . . and made the lab impossible to identify, without on-the-ground assets to eyeball it.

The Americans were walking into a town where one hundred men would be gunning for them, and they probably had no idea what waited for them there.

The Blackhawk circled north of Su Loc and settled down above the east side of the village, allowing Duke and his team to drop into a rice paddy.

They slogged through the water, climbed over the borders between paddies, and eventually wound their way onto a narrow path that led to the edge of the village. From this vantage point, Duke took a quick look around with his binoculars. Su Loc looked suspiciously dead for a village that should be waking up for another day. . . .

"Something's going on," he said.

Rip took the binoculars and saw for himself. "More like, nothing's going on."

"That's the point," Duke said. "This time of morning, people should be moving around. This is the kind of town that works from sunup to sundown. Why isn't there any activity at this hour?"

Rex shrugged. "Ghost town?"

Duke shook his head. "Our intel shouldn't be *that* far off—just two days ago, there were people here. Place was bustling. What the hell happened?"

Rex said, "Maybe intelligence got it wrong."

"Or maybe they bugged out," Rip said. "Lab and all."

"Operation like this," Duke said, considering that, "*could* pick up and move on, from time to time. . . ."

"Cool," Rip said. "That means we can just turn around and head on home."

"No," Duke said. "It means we have to check out that village, building by building."

They moved in one at a time, Duke first, Rip behind him, the others one by one. Slowly, they slogged toward the first building. They were only about five steps into their advance when the first shot rang out.

Edgerson, on the tail end of the line, took the round in the chest, knocking him backward.

"Cover!" Duke yelled, and they hightailed it for the jungle.

Rex and Duke cut to the fallen Edgerson, Rip staying with them to provide support fire as the rest of the world was now suddenly filled with the flash of tracers, the roar of guns, the whistle of bullets, and the smell of cordite.

From the jungle, the team returned fire as Duke and Rex each got Edgerson by an arm and dragged him toward the trees. Behind them, Rip sprayed bullets across the face of the nearest building, backpedaling after his friends.

They dove into the undergrowth, and got Edgerson behind a tree, where Rex could go over him carefully. The others kept up the return fire.

Edgerson groaned and Duke looked down to see sweat dripping off him, but no blood anywhere.

"Hit the vest?" Duke asked.

Rex nodded. "Slug impacted with enough force

to break his clavicle, though. Somebody's got to get him out."

"Somebody? Not you? You're our medic."

"And the rest of you may need me," Rex said. "Anyway, I have orders to carry out in that lab, if the damn thing's still here."

Duke thought he'd found a way to fulfill his promise to Ana without making Rex suspicious; but Rex was right, Duke did need him, and anyway the medic's top-secret orders were a priority of the mission. He'd have to honor his promise by keeping Rex as close as possible.

In the meantime, they had the tiny problem of being pinned down.

"I'll be okay," Edgerson said, his voice tight with pain, words emerging between gritted teeth. "You're going to need me, too—I can still shoot."

"Don't b.s. me, man," Duke said. "I can count on you?"

Edgerson nodded. "Ever let you down before?"

Knowing Edgerson was as good as his word, Duke moved back to where his men were firing sporadically at the nearest building.

"What's the story?" Duke asked.

"Maybe three guys shooting from windows," Peters said.

Duke took his first good look. Beyond their position yawned twenty yards of open ground between the edge of the jungle and the low-slung concrete building with a corrugated-metal roof, from which somebody was shooting.

The building—who knew what the hell it had once been, a grocery store maybe—was now nothing more than a well-built guard shack, its windows either broken or recently shot out by Able Team.

Rip said, "They've probably called in reinforcements already."

"You're right," Duke said. "We can't stay here."

To Peters, Rip said, "You *hear* that? Man said I was right about something."

The sniper smiled but said nothing. When the barrel of an AK–47 appeared in the window of the building, Peters let out his breath slowly as he pressed his eye to the scope and squeezed the trigger.

The barrel of the AK went up in the air, then disappeared inside.

Duke watched the window, but the barrel never reappeared. "Cover me," he said.

"You got it," Peters said.

"I'm comin' too," Rip said.

Duke shook his head. "Stay with him." He nodded toward Rex. "We need him when we find the lab."

"Got it," Rip said.

Duke took off left, getting as close to the left side of the building as possible without breaking cover, then threw himself behind a tree. He still had the twenty yards of open ground to cross—*nothing to it, but to do it. . . .*

After rising again, he sprinted across the open ground in a serpentine pattern. No shots near him—a good sign. That meant no one had come to back up the guards yet.

At the building, he stopped for maybe ten seconds to catch his breath, then was off again, scuttling along the wall below glassless windows. As he passed under each, he tossed in a grenade—no point in being subtle now. They were headed into a firefight with God only knew how many Eandokian soldiers.

The explosions came so close together, they felt and sounded like one large detonation, earth shaking beneath his shoes, damn near knocking him on his tail. Anyone within five klicks not raised by the gunfire sure as hell knew they were there now.

From here on, he thought, making his way back to the team, *it's gonna be one long bloody battle, finding that lab. . . .*

Gung Ho and Unit Alpha were double-timing their way through the jungle, the undergrowth slowing them down as they moved toward the village still maybe two klicks to the east. Snake Eyes, as usual, was on point, a couple hundred yards out.

They hustled along, wary of booby traps, despite their speed, and on guard for anyone they might run into. As they closed in on the village, Gung Ho was worried the Americans might beat them there, and run right into a hundred Eandokian regulars with automatic weapons.

They had advanced within half a klick of the west side of Su Loc when Gung Ho first heard the gunfire in the distance.

Damn!

A second later his wrist communicator vibrated, but Gung Ho already knew what Snake Eyes's message would be—the U.S. insertion team was already in the village!

Gung Ho knew that the Americans would call in an air strike, once they'd located the lab, and their scientist had done his thing. A precision smart bomb would then be deployed to take out just the laboratory, in hope civilian casualties could be minimized.

Gung Ho also knew Breaker could hack into the U.S. communications system and order the air strike himself. He preferred not to give an order that could result in the destruction of the entire village. More important, the American team would be lost too. That was not a price he was willing to pay. Yet.

As they closed in, the unit could hear gunfire intensifying on the other side. Gung Ho and his people moved even faster now.

He had a plan, or something close to one. . . .

If they could get to the village, Unit Alpha could serve as a diversion. Two teams fighting fifty men on opposite sides of the village seemed a better option than a single team fighting one hundred. Plus, if things went south, Gung Ho knew he could have the village leveled in a matter of minutes.

They were right outside Su Loc, still in the jungle, when a massive explosion detonated, a cloud of smoke and debris filling the air over on the other side of town.

Alpha Team quickly huddled up on the edge of the jungle.

"We need to make a fuss," Gung Ho said.

Heavy Duty arched an eyebrow. "A fuss?"

"Yeah—a big one." To Snake Eyes, Gung Ho added, "For once, silent and invisible is *not* a plus—get my drift?"

Snake Eyes nodded and took off toward the nearest building. Less than a minute later, gunfire erupted.

"Let's go help him out," Gung Ho shouted, and they were off.

They started by going house to house—door-to-door salesmen peddling machine-gun fire and hand grenades. Heavy D kicked in the door of a hut and blasted away, creating a huge racket—enough to bring a response, Gung Ho hoped, and a big one. . . .

Twenty Eandokian soldiers came around the corner of a building and chugged down a dirt street—guns at the ready and about to start firing at Heavy Duty and Gung Ho, when Scarlett and Breaker came out of doorways on either side, guns blazing.

The soldiers who'd managed to survive turned to beat a hasty retreat, but Snake Eyes appeared from nowhere behind them, the silent man's machine gun speaking volumes, cutting down soldiers right and left.

Gung Ho and Heavy D rushed forward, cleaning up the mess. All twenty soldiers were dead, but there would be more where they'd come from, and Unit Alpha still had no idea where the lab was. They'd cleared four buildings on the west side of town and found nothing, so far. At least they were making progress.

If they had to kill twenty enemy soldiers for every

block of "progress" they made, however, this would not only be a slow process but a costly one.

Gung Ho signaled to the team to round the corner. Another dirt road filled with shacks and shanties, men and women alike pouring out of the doors, each dressed as a civilian . . .

. . . yet each armed with an AK–47.

"Hit the dirt!" Gung Ho shouted, as the residents opened fire on them—the "civilians" obviously Eandokian regulars.

Unit Alpha dove for cover—Gung Ho, Scarlett, and Breaker into a house on the right side of the street, Heavy D and Snake Eyes in one across the dirt road.

"How do you like my plan so far?" Gung Ho asked Scarlett.

"My God," she said. "They're *everywhere*. . . ."

As they returned fire, Gung Ho used his wrist communicator to tell Snake Eyes to exit the building he shared with Heavy D, and do his deadly thing.

If they didn't find the lab soon, Gung Ho would have to call in the air strike, and hope the Americans all got out in one piece.

The JOEs, too.

Once the building exploded, Duke and his team circled back into the jungle. While the Eandokian soldiers rushed to their glorified guard shack, Able Team used the jungle as a way to come into town from a southeasterly direction. They still had plenty of buildings to search and—although they were now both hunters and hunted—Duke felt if they kept moving fast enough, they just might be able to keep this well-armed welcoming committee running in circles long enough for Able Team to pinpoint that damn lab. . . .

Oddly, he could hear gunfire, lots of it, from what sounded like the west side. Were the Eandokian soldiers shooting at his men, without having any idea where they were? Or were they shooting at someone else?

If so, *who* the hell?

They checked three more buildings on this block, each one empty. What bothered Duke was that the buildings, shanty houses, were not only vacant, but appeared not to have been lived in for quite some time.

That was when it hit him.

On its fringes at least, Su Loc *was* a ghost town. And Duke told himself that in a village whose citizenry had been replaced by soldiers, to protect a lab, that lab would not be situated anywhere but centrally.

Duke said, "We're in the wrong part of town."

Rip asked, "Where are we *supposed* to be?"

"Lab's got to be smack-dab in the middle," Duke said. "This is all gift wrap."

"I've received better presents. How the hell do we get there, and how do we know *what* building it is, in the middle of the damn town?"

"Both good questions," Duke said. "I know the answer to the first for sure and I think I know the answer to the second one, too." He addressed the other men. "Stearns, Bergman—set charges in this building and the last two as well. Set the timers for three minutes."

"We're already gone," Bergman said.

Once the charges were set, the team took off toward the center of town. They stuck to the edges of streets and alleys, hung in the shadows, did everything they could to avoid running into the Eandokian soldiers before the charges went off.

Even as they moved, Duke picked up the sound of gunfire from the west side. He still didn't know what was going on over there, but it sounded like someone was having one hell of a firefight.

For every soldier Unit Alpha put down, two more seemed to appear. Heavy D and his machine gun were keeping the Eandokians off his side of the street. Scarlett, Breaker, and Gung Ho were holding their own on their side, and Snake Eyes was out there doing what he did.

Problem was, even if they could get out of these buildings, there might not be any way to achieve their objective. Gung Ho started working out a plan for their escape and, more important, the timely destruction of the lab.

Into his wrist communicator, Gung Ho said, "All right, we're gonna bug out. Everybody get ready to move."

With Able Team trailing behind, Duke and Rip sprinted for the center of town. Enemy troops had spotted them and opened fire, but were far enough away that Able Team had the chance to outrun them. If they could stay ahead for a few seconds more. . . .

A giant *whoomp* announced a rising fireball. Most of the enemy soldiers at Able Team's back turned and ran toward the explosion, thinking (just as Duke had hoped) that another wave of invaders was back there. The rest of the enemy, however, continued to dog Able Team, firing all the way.

With Duke and Rip in the lead, the team rocketed down a bullet-pocked alley. Rex, kit bag over his shoulder and a .45 Colt auto on his hip, was just behind them, crouching as he ran. Stearns helped Edgerson while Bergman and Peters brought up the rear.

Duke and Rip stopped as the team went past. Both men took out grenades and lobbed them at the enemy soldiers following. They heard the explosions as they ran, not waiting to see how much damage they did.

Enemy fire still came their way and they returned it, moving fast, finally taking refuge behind a dead station wagon. Duke didn't know how far they'd run, but his lungs burned and his legs ached. Then he looked up and there it was . . .

. . . the corrugated-metal building that was their target, the entire reason for the mission, less than a hundred yards away now. Mercenaries on guard came around the side of the house in an assault that Duke and his men quickly took down.

Mercenaries, not Eandokian regulars—this *had* to be the place. . . .

Hunkered behind the car, Duke hand-signaled Stearns and Bergman to hit the front door. Machine guns at the ready, they rushed in, and no immediate sounds of gunfire were heard.

Enemy fire from in and around neighboring buildings continued, as well as from the jungle that choked this hellhole, and the insertion team returned fire. Duke still heard gunfire from the other side of town, but now it seemed to be fading, as if someone had retreated.

Duke paused to reload his machine gun, glancing at Rip beside him, who was doing the same. Rip looked a little overwhelmed.

"Double Bubble?" Duke asked his pal, offering him a piece of gum.

Rip took it and nodded his thanks.

"Always helps me," Duke said, and blew a bubble, popped it, and grinned at Rip. "You good?"

Rip, unwrapping the bubble gum, found a weak little grin. "Yeah. . . . Anybody tell you, you a fool?"

"Everybody, all the time."

They chewed their gum and waited, even as gunfire and explosions rocked the world.

"Where the hell are they?" Rip asked.

Just as he asked, Stearns appeared in the doorway of the shabby metal building. He signaled the "All clear," and Duke double-tapped Rex on the shoulder. The boyish brother of the woman Duke loved seemed small and kind of helpless.

So Duke put steely reassurance into his voice. "You're good to go, Rex. You don't find what you're after in that lab in four minutes, get the hell out. Because that piece-of-crap house won't be *standing* in five minutes—got it?"

"You sound sure of that."

"I just called in the air strike."

Rex swallowed. Nodded.

Duke gave him a smile and a pat on the back as Rex took off, running low, heading for the door. Duke kept his eyes on the man who'd been entrusted to him by both the U.S. Army and one Ana Lewis.

Stearns and Bergman stood just outside the building, guarding the entrance. Duke was satisfied that no one would be getting in to mess with his future brother-in-law. Still, he watched the building until the *whump* of mortars around him sent his eyes to the jungle.

But Rex was safely inside now, before the mortar rounds really started to hit, plowing the ground near the dead station wagon, sending dirt and dust and all manner of crap flying all around them.

Moving through the debris storm, Duke, Rip and the rest of the insertion team took new cover, behind another dead vehicle. Duke looked at his watch—four minutes until the air strike.

Bullets flew at them from rooftops and windows but mostly from the surrounding jungle, and Duke and Rip would catch glimpses of the enemy, lots of them, out there in the trees and growth, firing at them, and would pop up and return fire, as best they could. The best thing was to just try to keep their heads down.

Crouching behind the heap, Rip said, "Gotta level with you, bro!"

"I hate it when you level with me."

"Five minutes till air strike don't sound like that long."

"No it doesn't, and it's less than four now."

"Only I got a bad feeling it's gonna feel like five *hours.* . . ."

"No argument from me on that score," Duke said, and gritted his teeth and kept returning fire and reloading and returning fire.

But perhaps only two minutes had passed when, in the distance, they could hear the rumbling sonic roar of jet airplanes.

Duke and Rip traded startled looks.

"No," Duke said. "No, no, no . . . too soon! It's too damn *soon!*"

But there they were, F-16s in formation, streaking across a very blue sky.

Duke's eyes went to that sad-looking, shot-up corrugated-metal building.

"Rex!" he said into the com-link. "Get out *now!*"

He had promised her. He had promised Ana. . . .

Machine gun in hand, Duke ran from cover, charging toward the building, tracer fire and mortar explosions all around him. These he ignored, but the whistle of a bunker buster changed his plans, and he dove perhaps a moment before its *boom* flattened the pathetic building like a swatter does a fly.

At the same time, Duke was tossed as if God had discarded him, and he landed hard, though the physical pain barely registered, so terrible was the emotional hurt. He staggered to his feet, a jagged bloody rip cut in the flesh near his right eye.

Stumbling, he made his way toward the smoking, flaming rubble pile that had been a building. Rip and Peters helped Stearns and Bergman. The pair had run from the building as they heard the incoming bomb, but both men had caught shrapnel from the exploding corrugated-metal building. They would both be fine, but neither could walk well without assistance.

When the Blackhawk came sweeping low, ready for extraction, the tracer fire and explosions picked up in intensity, and black smoke was soon washing over Duke. He stood helpless in it, as if giving in to whatever fate had next for him . . .

. . . but then Rip was there, pulling his pal from the debris, saying, "Blackhawk's waiting, bro! Come on—we got wounded!"

"I can't."

"Nothing you can do for Rex. These are our guys who *can* be helped. Come on!"

And gunfire burst all around them, as Rip pulled Duke away from the ruins of the lab house, toward the waiting chopper.

They all got aboard and the Blackhawk lifted off without catching any hits. As the chopper banked away from the building, Duke looked down at the smoking heap of the lab, no longer a building now, just a grave, a twisted metal marker for Rex Lewis.

Gung Ho prayed the Americans had made it out, but he couldn't have waited a moment longer. The U.S. radio operator he talked to said that another member of the team had just called in the strike for five minutes. Gung Ho had overridden the order, telling the operator, "Now! Now! *Now*!"

The F–16s that had been flying on standby were alerted and the bunker buster had been delivered.

Gung Ho hoped it was sent to the right address and that the visitors had gotten onto their chopper and gotten the hell away.

He hoped. And prayed.

CHAPTER TWELVE

Rainy Mourning

Bangkok, Thailand

If the mission had gone well, General Hawk would have waited for debriefing until Unit Alpha got back to the Pit. Since there'd been something of a hitch, he had jetted to the nearest feasible point outside Su Loc.

In a hangar at U-Tapao airbase south of Bangkok, on the gulf of Thailand, the general sat at a small table, drumming the fingers of one hand, reading Breaker's report, which had been sent from the chopper bringing back Unit Alpha. In camouflage fatigues today, black boots, and a black beret, Hawk by all appearances was the U.S. general he'd been before taking command of G.I. JOE.

In similar fatigues, which did little to camouflage her lithe, shapely form, Cover Girl approached Hawk to say, "I've got the initial incident report from the U.S. insertion team."

"What does it say?"

"One dead; three wounded, none seriously. The lab was destroyed. No civilian casualties, since of course there were no real civilians in Su Loc. The

U.S. team is estimating Eandokian casualties at between thirty and forty, though obviously they have
no notion how many our unit took out. The Americans also mention a team of a dozen mercenaries
they dealt with."

Hawk frowned, gesturing with the hard-copy
file. "Breaker's report says nothing about mercs."

"No, sir. Our team saw only Eandokian regulars. Able Team took out another twenty-five of
those, at least—as much as three-quarters of the
enemy force, as well as the mercenaries, were killed
by the combined teams. And this doesn't count any
taken out by the bunker buster."

Hawk nodded. "At least the objective was accomplished—the lab is history."

"Yes, sir. But we still don't know for sure what
they were up to."

Hawk said, "Our intel sources are confident the
scientists were working on developing enhance-
ment drugs that would lead to super soldiers. Of
course, the myth of super soldiers has been around
since the beginning of time . . . and I would like to
see that it remains a myth for as long as possible."

"Yes, sir."

"We are left with a disturbing reality—those top-
flight scientists, presumably killed when the lab exploded, were in *someone's* hire. A banana republic
like San Sebastiao or its Asian counterpart Su Loc
could not fund research this sophisticated. Certainly a small-time arms dealer like Chernitz isn't
capable of such an effort. Who *is*?"

"Do you have a theory, sir?"

"Less than a theory, more than a hunch—I can

almost *feel* it out there, a deadly new player on the world stage, coiled like a venomous snake in the shadows, waiting to strike."

"A nation, sir?"

"No. Something bigger. What exactly, I don't know . . . yet. I only know that it represents the kind of threat G.I. JOE was created to stop."

Outside, a chopper was setting down on the tarmac. Hawk, hearing the craft come in, went to meet them, Cover Girl trailing respectfully.

The G.I. JOE unit walked toward the hangar, with little of the usual spring in their step, their exhaustion palpable—these were warriors carrying the filth of battle, encrusted with caked dirt and dried blood. The world around them was gray, the late morning overcast but not cool—humid as hell, in fact.

Still, all five were alive and none the worse for wear, which improved Hawk's mood. These were professional soldiers, the best of the best from nations around the world. Yet in a certain sense, they were his children, and he wanted them safe.

At sight of Hawk, Gung Ho barked, "Ten-*hut*!"

Despite their exhaustion, the team snapped to and saluted.

Hawk returned their salute. "Welcome back, Unit Alpha. At ease."

"Thank you, sir," Gung Ho said, as the team relaxed from attention.

Hawk asked, "So intel was wrong—it was a ghost town with guns?"

Gung Ho nodded. "Two full platoons."

"That," Hawk said, "plus mercenaries."

Gung Ho frowned. "Sir, we didn't see anything but regular army . . . either in uniform or disguised civilian attire."

Scarlett said, "Though their guns were kind of a giveaway."

Hawk said, "Mercenaries were guarding the lab. The American team took them out."

"And the lab itself?"

Hawk nodded. "The air strike knocked it out."

"Least that much went right."

"At a price—apparently the Army scientist was inside the lab when it went."

In the hangar, Hawk and Gung Ho took opposite sides of the table, Cover Girl next to the general, the rest of Unit Alpha scattered about the hangar. Medical staff checked them out while Hawk and Gung Ho went over the mission in detail, Cover Girl recording it.

By the time the pair was done, the other members had been bandaged and cleaned up. Hawk and Gung Ho joined them in the corner of the hangar, where they'd received medical attention— most were seated in simple folding chairs, though Heavy Duty was pacing, working out a kink in his neck.

"The Able Team man who didn't make it," Gung Ho said to his teammates, "I take responsibility for him." His face was ashen. "Seems by moving up that air strike, even a few minutes, I got one of 'em killed."

Nobody liked hearing that.

Then the general said, "That's one way to look at it."

Their eyes went to their commander.

"Another way," Hawk said to Gung Ho, but for everyone's benefit, "is by moving up the air strike, you saved lives."

"How is that, sir?"

"With the odds you and the U.S. team were facing, if you'd waited for the air strike to happen on time, none of you might be here now. You were twelve against one hundred or more. Good as you are, and as good as the U.S. team might be, those are still steep odds. I know we try for a zero casualty rate, but sometimes trading one life for eleven is an acceptable sacrifice."

"We know that, sir," Scarlett said. No one would argue that the lovely redhead didn't know more about odds and math than the rest of them. "It's just . . . we don't have to *like* it."

"No," Hawk admitted, "no, you don't. And I have only one other order for you today."

All eyes perked.

"A week's leave," the general said. "You've earned it."

They were all smiles, hearing that. But their usual response of "Yo, JOES!" did not come—a man had died, and however small a failure that might be in the greater victory, a failure it remained.

Able Team had been out of Eandok for two days. There'd been no news at all on CNN International about Su Loc. With three days R & R to spend in Bangkok, Duke had split off from the partying-inclined Rip, whiling most of it away locked in his hotel, with only mediocre room service and old American TV shows dubbed in Thai to keep him company.

Tonight, instead of brooding in his room, he was brooding in a bar. Not normally a power drinker, Duke had shotgunned a couple when he first got there, then slowed his pace, going from straight rum to rum and Coke. An hour later, he was nursing his fourth drink, an anonymous American in a plain black T-shirt, black cargo pants, and black combat boots. He carried no ID, little money, and other than a tiny black box, nothing else.

This dimly lit dump was in a part of town tourists never saw, a long bar running down one side, tables and chairs squatting across the shallow, wide room. The joint was pretty well packed, most tables full with only a couple bar stools empty.

A jukebox played Thai popular music, familiar American-style rock accompanied by singsong off-key caterwauling; but the other patrons seemed perfectly content with it. The place reeked of booze, cheap perfume, puke, and urine.

Sitting there, nursing his drink, staring at the tiny black box resting before him on the bar, Duke couldn't think of anything beyond Ana and his broken promise to her. What could he possibly say that would inspire her forgiveness?

The air strike showing early hadn't been his fault, but that had no bearing here. He knew only that the woman he loved had entrusted him with the most precious thing in her life, her brother, and he had failed her—Rex had been killed. There was nothing he could say, nothing he could do that would make this thing right.

Behind him, a woman started swearing in Thai, in one of the many Asian dialects he'd mastered at the Army's Special Languages School. Duke turned to see two white men and two Thai women at the table directly behind him.

The bigger man, a potbellied, sweaty ape with a two-day beard and a thatch of unruly black hair, wore a faded T-shirt and filthy dungarees. The smaller guy wore a button-down shirt and greasy khakis.

The two women were obviously prostitutes—one in a short skirt and spaghetti-strapped top that barely held in her assets, the other sheathed in a black Naugahyde jumpsuit that had to be hotter than a sauna.

The ape had hold of the spaghetti-strap gal by the arm.

Now Duke knew why she was swearing—negotiations were not going well.

The woman tried to free herself but the ape was too strong. The bartender barked for them to either calm down or take it outside, and finally the hooker wrenched away. Still, she remained at the table with the simian. Evidently, negotiations would continue.

Duke returned his attention to the black box. He finished his drink and ordered another one. Before the bartender could step away, a voice next to Duke said, "I'll have one of the same. I'll catch this round."

Glancing at his benefactor, Duke said, "Thanks, anyway."

"I insist," the man said, plopping onto the stool next to Duke. He was pushing thirty, tall, solidly built, with buzz-cut brown hair, blue eyes, and a no-nonsense jaw.

The guy's black Polo, black slacks, and rubber-soled loafers were not dissimilar to Duke's attire—military or CIA, he figured, but probably the former. Something about him said fighting man.

"Do I know you?" Duke asked.

He shook his head. "Not yet."

The guy didn't seem to be hitting on him, or even looking for another American for conversation. The bartender brought the drinks and set them down.

The man in black paid.

Duke nodded his thanks and sipped the drink.

Behind him, the woman started blathering again and when Duke turned, the ape again had her by the damn arm. Duke was about to intercede when the bartender stepped back in, and told the guy to either settle things with her or get the hell out.

The ape glared at the bartender, but said nothing and released the woman again. She sat down and the negotiations took on a more peaceful tenor.

The guy in black asked, "Mind if I ask what's in the box?"

"My reward."

"For what?"

"For getting a guy killed."

The man said nothing.

"There was another box like this," Duke said, wiggling a finger at the small black object. "It had a ring in it. I'll probably get that back, though. In the mail maybe."

"But *that's* not a ring."

"No. Like I said before, it's a reward. I got a guy killed and this is what they gave me." He raised the lid on the black box and held it out so the guy could see the shiny captain's bars inside. "I get a man killed, and get a goddamn promotion."

Gung Ho tried to think of something to say that might ease the pain of the man he'd come at Hawk's behest to recruit; but he realized there was nothing to say. The teammate killed on the Su Loc mission was not an ordinary casualty, but someone close to Hauser. Though Duke seemed solid G.I. JOE material to Gung Ho, now was not the time. The guy was in too much pain, in too dark a place. . . .

And right now the young man might view an offer to join G.I. JOE as just one more "reward" for getting his friend killed.

"You know what they say," Gung Ho said easily, "about time healing wounds."

"Don't know if that covers a wound this—"

Before Duke got any further, the sound of a heavy slap behind them was quickly followed by a scream and wail. Both men turned to see the spaghetti-strap woman on the floor, the ape standing over her, with a big grin saying he was really proud of himself. . . .

Instantly off his stool, Duke wiped the ape's grin away with a straight right hand that dropped the bastard to the floor next to the woman, who stopped wailing and began beating tiny hard fists into the ugly mug's ugly mug.

Behind Duke, the ape's smaller partner came out

of his chair, the snick of a switchblade warning the soldier, who had very little room to turn, and none to kick out at his attacker.

Instead, Duke ducked as the man lunged with the knife, then launched him over a shoulder into two tables mid-room, for a landing that brought both tables down in a V, with the guy between them, splashed with spilled beer and booze, as other patrons screamed and yelled in fear and protest respectively, while the knife skittered away somewhere.

That should have been the end of it, Gung Ho thought, but a ring of patrons formed around Duke, who they clearly viewed as a troublemaking outsider. Behind Gung Ho, the bartender was jabbering away, and across the room the jukebox seemed suddenly louder with its discordant clatter. Gung Ho watched as bar patrons came at Duke in waves. Chairs flew, bodies tumbled, and women shrilled as the melee grew into a near riot.

One dumb S.O.B. even had the bad sense to try Gung Ho. A beer bottle cracked over the man's ear convinced him to take a nap at Gung Ho's feet. Otherwise, the G.I. JOE team leader did not enter the fray, simply watching and marveling as Duke, in the middle, fought off attack after attack.

The Hauser boy was at least half-drunk. Imagine him *sober*!

One guy rushed Duke with a broken beer bottle and Duke ducked the thrust, grabbing the man's wrist as it went by, twisting it with a hard jerk that made the bottle drop and bones break. The guy began to scream, adding a baritone to the choir of soprano and alto shrieking.

Two more roughnecks came at Duke, throwing kung fu punches and kicks. These Duke fended off easily, backing toward the bar, people getting out of his way. This pair of attack dogs thought they had Duke cornered, but just as they moved in, he leapt onto the bar, kicked one in the face, knocking him unconscious, then dove onto the other one, driving him to the floor, Duke pummeling him with punches the entire time. After pushing himself up off the man, Duke delivered one last hard right cross, and the attacker was out cold.

Gung Ho watched as the ape finally knocked the woman aside, rose, and came up behind Duke, who was just pushing himself to his feet. The ape draped himself over Duke's shoulders, his arm going around Duke's neck in a choke hold. The brute straightened, Duke's feet coming off the floor.

Duke's eyes bulged and he elbowed the guy in the ribs, once, twice, a third time, to no apparent effect as the ape kept on choking him. The new captain's face turned red, then purple. Gung Ho was halfway off his bar stool when Duke kicked back and caught the ape in the jewels.

At first, nothing happened, then the ape lowered Duke to the floor, though managing to maintain his choke hold.

With one leg planted on the floor, Duke kicked back again and this time, the ape yelped and let go of Duke, who spun and hit the bastard with a quick one-two, then stepped back and swung a roundhouse kick that nearly took the guy's face off, dropping him unconscious to the filthy floor.

Another patron came at Duke, who grabbed the guy by his shirt front, lifting and throwing him over the bar, to crash into the back wall in a cacophony of breaking glasses and exploding liquor bottles.

Three more were heading his way, but the piercing whistles of policemen pouring through the front door froze them. Duke stood, breath heaving, reaching over only to retrieve his black box before the cops grabbed and cuffed him.

Hauser was G.I. JOE material all right, of this Gung Ho had no doubt; but not right now—and that was the opinion he would report back to General Hawk. Too much anger, too much pain in the boy. Showing his ID to the police, Gung Ho exited the bar just as Duke was loaded into a paddy wagon.

On a dreary wet afternoon, a steady drizzle falling at Arlington National Cemetery near Washington, D.C., mourners gathered before the flag-draped casket of Major Rex Lewis. Ana, her raincoat a somber black, stood alone but for a single soldier shielding her with an umbrella—no family, and no Duke, either, as she stared at her brother's memorial. A minister stood nearby.

From a hill deep in the cemetery, Duke watched as the other members of Able Team—Peters, Stearns, Bergman, Edgerson, Ripcord, and others—fired three volleys skyward. As they did, an Arlington honor guard lifted the flag from Rex's casket and folded it with mournful ceremony. The last man stepped forward and presented the folded flag to Ana.

After handing their weapons to the honor guard, each Able Team member passed Ana and offered their condolences. Rip was last and Duke wished he was close enough to hear. He was certain Ana was asking Rip why he wasn't there, and Duke felt bad for putting his buddy in that situation. Soon Ana—folded American flag in her grasp—stood alone before her brother's metal casket, the other mourners gone but for the soldier shielding her with the umbrella.

Not enough of Rex's body had survived to even justify a body bag, and the casket was as empty as Duke felt, watching the woman he loved grieve alone. He had let her down.

They shared a common grief, felt an agony obvious in both their faces, but they could never again share anything else.

Climbing aboard his vintage Indian motorcycle, Duke gunned the engine to life. Without approaching her, he drove away and out of her life, figuring it was the kindest thing he could do, and hoping he was not just being a coward.

But Ana knew he was there.

She'd heard, in the distance, the distinctive sound of his Indian. She had ridden it many times, him in front, her in back, arms around his waist. She could put her ear against his back and hear his heart beat as they motored down backroads and highways alike.

That had been a different time, and a different them. Why he wasn't here at her side was something she would never understand. He loved her, she knew that. She loved him. Her brother's death had been Rex's own fault—*Rex* was the one who volunteered, who'd simply *had* to get out of the lab and into the field. . . .

Looking down at the coffin, she felt sick—her anger for her brother blotting out her love for him, leaving only the wrenching sense of loss, and a loss not just for Rex.

She pressed the flag to her bosom, her left hand still adorned with the diamond Duke had given her—the flag and the ring, symbols of the two men she had loved the most, and who had both let her down. Neither was here with her. Rex, at least, had an excuse.

She walked away in the rain from the graveside, her escort protecting her with the black umbrella, and she could still hear the motorcycle there in the distance, as Duke rode out of her life.

She wondered if they would ever be together again—if either one could put it all aside and have the courage to face the other. She felt for Duke a mix of hate and love similar to what she bore for Rex.

Walking back to the waiting hearse, she made herself a promise—when the time was right, she and Duke would meet again.

READY FOR MORE?

Don't miss the
official novelization
of the blockbuster film!

by Max Allan Collins
Story by Michael Gordon,
Stuart Beattie, and Stephen Sommers
Screenplay by Stuart Beattie,
David Elliot, and Paul Lovett
Based on Hasbro's G.I. Joe® Characters

Available Summer 2009 everywhere books are sold!

www.delreybooks.com
www.gijoemovie.com
www.hasbro.com